# A MURDEROUS VALENTINE
## THE ADMIRAL SHACKLEFORD MYSTERIES
### BOOK ONE

BEVERLEY WATTS

Copyright © 2017 BaR Publishing

All rights reserved. No part of this publication may be reproduced, stored or transmitted in any form or by any means, electronic, mechanical, photocopying, recording, scanning or otherwise without written permission from the publisher.

It is illegal to copy this book, post it to a website, or distribute it by any other means without permission.

This novel is entirely a work of fiction. The names, characters and incidents portrayed in it are the work of the author's imagination. Any resemblance to actual persons, living or dead, events or localities is entirely coincidental.

BaR Publishing has no responsibility for the persistence or accuracy of URL's for external or third party Internet Websites referred to in this publication and does not guarantee that any content on such Websites is, or will remain, accurate or appropriate.

Designations used by companies to distinguish their products are often claimed as trademarks. All brand names and product names used in this book and on its cover are trade names, service marks, trademarks and registered trademarks of their respective owners. The publishers and the book are not associated with any product or vendor mentioned in this book. None of the companies referenced within the book have endorsed the book.

Cover Design by Covers by Karen

*To my mum, whose love of a good cozy mystery led me to want to write one, and to my husband Rob who kept me hard at it...*

## CHAPTER 1

Retired Admiral Charles Shackleford was sitting on his customary seat at the bar of his favourite watering hole, ruminating into his pint of real ale. His long standing, not to mention long suffering friend Jimmy Noon was sitting silently next to him, and his aging Springer Spaniel Pickles was snoring on the floor in between them.

All was well with the world. Or at least it should be. With a heartfelt sigh, the Admiral took a long draft of his pint before admitting to himself that he was bored.

'Is there something wrong Sir,' Jimmy asked his former commanding officer with slight trepidation. His foreboding was well warranted, having been a reluctant participant in many of the Admiral's harebrained schemes for nigh on fifty years. Although he had to admit, if only privately, that Charles Shackleford's penchant for interfering in matters that were none of his business had definitely increased over the last couple. The small man sipped his pint and sighed. He'd faithfully followed Charles Shackleford's orders to the letter when they were both in uniform, but somehow he'd never got out of the habit, even though they'd both been retired for fifteen years.

Jimmy took another swallow, knowing that the Admiral would spit out his problem when he was good and ready. After another five minutes of silence, he glanced down at his watch. He'd told his wife Emily that he'd be home for dinner by six. He needed to hurry this along a bit.

'Would you like a packet of crisps Sir?' he asked mildly, hoping that the thought of his stomach might encourage his old friend to get on with it. When there was no response, he sighed and took another sip of his beer.

Charles Shackleford finally shook his head mournfully. 'The thing is Jimmy lad, I've been instrumental in improving the lives of so many...' Jimmy spluttered into his pint, very nearly spilling the whole lot over Pickles' head. The Admiral frowned at the small man coughing and spluttering into his glass. What the bloody hell was wrong with him?

'That's not the first time you've wasted a perfectly good pint of beer Jimmy. I'm beginning to think a visit to a scab lifter might be in order.' Clobbering his friend vigorously on the back, the Admiral waved at the bar maid to bring them both another pint.

After a few seconds, Jimmy recovered enough to take another drink which helped considerably. 'Please carry on Sir,' he wheezed.

The Admiral frowned and returned to his pint. 'As I was saying,' he continued pompously, 'So many lives have taken a turn for the better due to my...' he paused and patted Jimmy on the shoulder condescendingly, adding, 'Of course I mean *our* intervention Jimmy boy.'

The small man shook his head in denial. 'You can't blame me for all the chaos you've caused Sir,' he protested.

'But now,' the Admiral shook his head, completely ignoring Jimmy's objection, 'Now things are just... well everything's just tedious.' Charles Shackleford exhaled noisily and stared back down into his pint, thinking back over the fun and games of the last two years.

It had been a manic couple of years and no mistake. First his daughter Victory had gone and snagged herself the most famous actor in the world – all due to yours truly, it had to be said.

Then there was the little shenanigans involving the Thai prostitute. Fortunately that misunderstanding had been resolved to everyone's satisfaction. And as if that wasn't enough, Tory had then gone and married her actor and promptly given him his first carpet crawler.

'What about Mabel?' Jimmy interrupted his ruminations by sticking a packet of crisps under his nose. 'Aren't you happy together?' The Admiral took a handful and chomped thoughtfully.

Was he happy with Mabel? They'd been living together since Victory had left, but the elderly widow had so far refused to marry him, saying that once was enough and she was too independent to tie herself to an old dinosaur like him. Cheek of it.

He shook his head slowly. 'I think it's lost its sparkle Jimmy lad,' he whispered in a rare moment of candour.

'Perhaps you need to inject a bit of romance,' Jimmy offered, moved by his old friend's admission. 'Valentine's Day's coming up, why don't you take Mabel out for a slap up dinner? Women love to be wooed on Valentine's Day. It's in their genes or something. I'm taking Emily away for the weekend,' he finished proudly. The Admiral looked across at his friend thoughtfully.

'You might be on to something there Jimmy boy,' he murmured, 'We haven't been out the house since the bloody high jinks at Christmas. Where are you taking Emily?'

Jimmy heard the alarm bells ringing inside his head, but his mouth unaccountably moved of its own volition. 'The Two Bridges up on Dartmoor. You know that lovely old country inn with all the log fires and beams and stuff.'

'Bloody hell Jimmy, that's in the middle of nowhere. Dartmoor in February? I'd rather have my tonsils removed with a set of pliers.'

Jimmy released a breath he didn't know he was holding, relief swamping him.

'Well there are lots of nice cosy places to eat in Dartmouth,' he said enthusiastically, 'Why don't you surprise Mabel? That's another thing women love. Surprises…'

∞∞∞

The Admiral couldn't believe he was doing this. Bloody Dartmoor in February. Still, Jimmy had been right about the whole surprises thing. When he'd told Mabel to pack a bag because he was taking her somewhere nice, she'd actually squealed, then promptly burst into tears. Operation *Cary Grant* was definitely a goer.

They'd be giving Jimmy and Emily another surprise too when they arrived at the Two Bridges. The Admiral nodded to himself in satisfaction at the thought of their friends' delight when he and Mabel poled up.

Hefting Mabel's suitcase into the boot of the car, he looked up at the weather with a slight frown. The sky looked like a dirty dishcloth. Perfect weather for snow. Luckily the forecaster had said it would only be a smattering for south Devon. He couldn't help but shudder and sympathize with the poor buggers up north who were likely to be knee deep in the stuff by the morning.

Satisfied that everything they needed for a romantic night away was safely stowed in the car, he went back inside to call Victory. His daughter had offered to keep Pickles overnight. There was nothing more guaranteed to put a damper on any amorous goings on than a wet nose panting down your pyjama top.

'What time are you coming to pick up the hound?'

'Hello to you too dad.' As always, his daughter's sarcasm was completely lost on him as the Admiral continued, 'I don't want to be getting off too late, driving round bloody Dartmoor in the dark is not my idea of a jaunt.'

Tory had to agree, especially as her father's erratic driving skills had resulted in him being on first name terms with most of the traffic police in Devon. She felt sorry for Mabel and wondered for the hundredth time what on earth had made her father decide on a romantic weekend away in the wilds of Dartmoor. In February. He usually never went further than the Ship.

Sighing, she dropped her bombshell. 'I'm sorry dad, I can't have Pickles overnight. We think Isaac's come down with chicken pox. I called The Two Bridges and they're totally dog friendly so you're just going to have to take Pickles with you.'

Unaccustomed concern for his grandson warred briefly with disappointment that Operation *Cary Grant* was already going up the swanny and they hadn't even left the house yet. With a heartfelt sigh, he surrendered to the inevitable and told Tory to give Isaac a big kiss for him.

Half an hour later they were off. If the traffic wasn't too heavy, it would take them about an hour to get to the Two Bridges. Pickles was ensconced on Mabel's knee and unaccountably the elderly matron hadn't been too unhappy when she found out the spaniel would be coming with them. All in all, Operation *Cary Grant* was back on track.

Smiling to himself, the Admiral envisaged the light-hearted meeting with Jimmy and Emily to come. It had been obvious that Jimmy had been hinting when he'd told the Admiral about his Valentine's Day plans. They'd been friends for so long, the Admiral could read his former master at arms like a book. He just hoped that Jimmy appreciated the sacrifice he was making.

The first flakes of snow began drifting across the bonnet just as they passed the sign for the Dartmoor National Park. Mabel looked anxiously out of the window.

'Don't worry old girl, it's not going to settle.' The Admiral patted her arm as they headed up onto the bleak surroundings of the moor itself. 'We'll be snug as bugs in a rug in no time with a pint and a nice glass of sherry before dinner.'

By the time they pulled into the car park at The Two Bridges, the snow had stopped as the Admiral predicted. There were lots of cars, including a mini bus being unloaded by a group of laughing youngsters. The Admiral frowned. He'd been assured that the whole evening would be an intimate gathering of around thirty guests.

'I hope it's not going to be too noisy,' Mabel murmured worriedly as she got out of the car and put the reluctant spaniel on the ground. The Admiral was too busy staring at a large Rolls Royce Bentley parked in the corner of the car park to answer, and glancing round he realised that several of the cars were definitely from the upper end of the market. He wondered how Jimmy would fare, mixing with the upper echelons of society. Never mind, he'd give his old friend some pointers, make sure the small man didn't make any unforgivable gaffs. It was a good job he had a former Admiral to show him the ropes.

'Come along Mabel, let's go and get ourselves settled. We've got a couple of hours before dinner, so we've got time for a quick nap…'

# CHAPTER 2

The young lady on reception checked them in with instructions to be in the dining room at seven for half past. Apparently this was so that the guests could meet up with The Cast and get a feel for the evening.

The Admiral had no idea what she was talking about but shrugged it off and asked sotto voce if Mr. and Mrs. Noon had arrived. The young lady – Karen was written on her jacket – glanced down at her book and nodded. Apparently Jimmy and Emily had arrived half an hour ago. With mounting excitement, the Admiral grabbed Pickles' lead, took Mabel's arm and followed the concierge to their room.

The four poster bed was simply huge and the bathroom sported a walk in shower as well as a Jacuzzi style bath that would easily take both him and Mabel providing they actually managed to get in and out… The Admiral wondered if he might persuade his partner to indulge, but then, looking down at his corpulent figure, thought better of it.

All in all though, he was very satisfied that he'd made the right decision. Mabel was in raptures and the bottle of bubbly sitting on ice would make a nice start to the evening.

Gallantly he popped the cork on the Champagne and poured them both a large glass. 'To us Mabel old girl,' he said, overcome by the moment. Mabel gasped as the bubbles went up her nose and in no time at all, she was giggling like a school girl. Maybe a romantic bath together wasn't beyond the realms of possibility. He could put lots of bubbles in to hide any unsavoury bits. Feeling like a modern day Don Juan, he kissed Mabel firmly and disappeared into the bathroom.

After turning on the taps, he left the hot water to cascade into the cavernous tub and turned his attention to the little bottles on the side. Unfortunately he wasn't wearing his glasses, but he wasn't about to ruin the moment by hunting round for them. He sniffed the contents of each bottle carefully, then, throwing caution to the winds, poured them all into the bath which was now filling up nicely.

As he went back into the bedroom, the Admiral noted that Pickles had wasted no time in making himself comfortable on the beautiful tartan bedspread. But still firmly in Latin lover mode, Charles Shackleford was determined that the dog would be relegated to the couch when he and his beloved went to bed.

With a flourish, he took Mabel's hand and led her into the bathroom. 'Your bath awaits my lady,' he declared boldly, waving towards the whirlpool of soap suds which were admittedly a little higher than he'd anticipated. Hurriedly he went to turn off the taps. At this rate it wouldn't only be the unsavoury bits that were hidden; they'd have difficulty seeing each other at all.

Rolling up his sleeve, he dipped in his hand. Perfect. 'I'll leave you to your ablutions lovely lady,' he murmured, totally on a roll now, 'And with your permission, I'll rejoin you shortly.'

Ignoring Mabel's bemused expression, he backed out of the room and shut the door. Then, feeling as though he was eighteen again, he hastily stripped off to his vest and pants. At the end of the day, he didn't want to give the old girl a coronary.

After five minutes he put his ear to the door, and satisfied he could hear splashing noises, he threw it open, causing Mabel to give a small startled scream. Luckily she was firmly ensconced in the water, surrounded by a mountain of bubbles. Not quite sure what to do next, the Admiral decided that on this occasion, speed was definitely his best option. Quickly pulling off his underwear, he clambered over the edge of the bath, lost his footing and slid like a virgin ship into the water.

'Would you like me to scrub your back dear?' he sputtered as he surfaced, spitting out soap suds. Leaning forward helpfully, he accidentally sat on a button situated next to the plug. A sudden loud whirring nearly frightened the life out of him. 'What the bloo...' The words died as the water began churning and the bubbles slowly rose higher and higher.

'Charlie...' Mabel's screech came somewhere to the left of him. How had he managed to turn round? The steam in the bathroom was increasing along with the bubbles and it was becoming impossible to see anything at all.

All of a sudden Mabel rose from the suds, just like Aphrodite. For a few seconds all the Admiral could do was stare in awe. This had truly never happened to him before. Unfortunately, all too soon his beloved brought him back down to earth with a resounding thump as she threw a bar of soap at his head yelling, 'Pull out the damn plug you idiot.'

Struggling in vain to get the soap out of his eye, the Admiral felt around the bottom trying to find the plug hole. The foam was now well over his head and he couldn't help but wonder if death by bubble bath was actually possible.

Just when all seemed lost, he finally found it and wrenched the plug out, feeling like Indiana Jones. Holding it aloft, he waved it triumphantly at Mabel as the water slowly began to subside.

Now all they had to do was get out...

∞∞∞

Well it had to be said Operation *Cary Grant* was in danger of ending before it had actually started. By the time he managed to lever Mabel out of the bath, he felt less like Indiana Jones and more like Captain Ahab landing Moby Dick. Not to mention his back was playing up something chronic.

Still it was nothing a short lie down wouldn't put right he was sure, and glancing over at Mabel snoring lightly beside him, he reflected that maybe tomorrow morning the walk in shower might be more advisable.

An hour and a half later they were both dressed and ready to go. The Admiral had brought his Mess Undress to wear in lieu of a dinner jacket, for two reasons. One, he thought he looked pretty bloody chipper in his uniform (once an Admiral, always an Admiral…) and two – well it was cheaper.

Staring at himself in the full length mirror, Charles Shackleford had to admit he still cut a fine figure. While it was true that his tailcoat didn't actually do up, his cummerbund fortunately covered the buttons that were straining on the front of his shirt.

'Are you going to take Pickles out to do his business before we go down?' Mabel's voice was clipped indicating that she hadn't yet forgiven him for manhandling her out of the bath.

The Admiral winced and hurriedly went to pour her another glass of Champagne. Although she remarked tartly that she'd had enough of bubbles to last her a lifetime, she nevertheless took the proffered glass, giving the Admiral reason to hope that her temper would improve as the evening got under way.

Clipping on Pickles' lead, the Admiral headed out into the corridor. Unfortunately he couldn't remember which way they'd come when being shown to their room.

'Place is like a bloody warren,' he mumbled to himself as he doubled back for the second time. Finally he found a small door which opened on to a narrow staircase leading down. Reasoning that it was going the right way at least, he pulled Pickles through the door and led the spaniel down the stairs.

The passage turned a sharp right at the bottom, but just as the Admiral reached the last step, he heard raised voices. Frowning he pulled Pickles back and stuck his head round the corner to see a man and a woman who were clearly arguing.

'You did this to me. You deserve everything you damn well get.' the woman said, through gritted teeth.

The man's response was to laugh nastily and shake his head. 'My dear girl, I assure you that I have nothing to concern myself with. Do your worst. But remember…' His voice lowered as he leaned forward and the Admiral was unable to hear his words. Whatever he said was enough to make the woman step back hastily.

For a couple of seconds she looked as though she would burst into tears, but instead, she turned her back and flounced away leaving the man standing staring after her.

For reasons he couldn't quite fathom, the Admiral remained at the bottom of the stairs and watched as the man pulled a mobile phone from his pocket, looked down, and after muttering about the damn lack of signal, headed in the direction of his companion.

Pickles' soft whining brought him back to the matter at hand. Bending down, he gave the dog a quick pat and cautiously stepped into the narrow corridor wondering what the couples' argument had been about.

To his relief the passageway opened up into a larger hallway leading towards the public areas, and as he headed towards the main entrance, he glanced around the lobby but the couple were nowhere to be seen.

Standing shivering while Pickles made a big thing of doing his business, the Admiral wondered again what the couple had been arguing about. The woman had been clearly angry, but scared. He frowned. They'd both been dressed in nineteen twenties costume. Well at least the woman had. The man had been wearing a tux. Were they going to the Valentine's dinner? If so, it was a pretty bloody strange way to start a romantic evening.

Something about their whole encounter unsettled him. He saw the woman's face again in his head, the anger, but overriding that, the fear. What had she been afraid of?

His ruminating was cut short as he suddenly realized that it had started snowing again. 'Bugger,' he muttered to himself looking up at the dark sky, then looking back at the welcoming lights of the old country inn, he shook off his sense of foreboding and headed back into the warmth.

# CHAPTER 3

Jimmy had been looking forward to this weekend away for months. He'd managed to keep it a surprise from Emily right up until the last minute, and once he'd broken the news, they'd spent a delightful week planning their costumes for the nineteen twenties house party theme. Of course things had very nearly gone pear shaped when he'd admitted to the Admiral that he was taking Emily away for Valentine's weekend.

He recalled his feeling of relief when his friend had completely poo-pooed the idea. God knows what Emily would have said if the old goat had decided to come – he'd probably be spending the night on the floor. Chuckling to himself, he wondered what the Admiral had finally come up with – most likely he'd be taking Mabel down to The Ship…

∞∞∞∞

To be fair, Jimmy's reaction to seeing him and Mabel wasn't exactly what the Admiral had expected. In fact Emily and Mabel didn't look particularly happy either. And to top it all, Jimmy and his wife were dressed like nineteen twenties gangsters.

'What the bloody hell are you wearing Jimmy?' The Admiral as usual did not mince words.

'Jimmy didn't mention that you and Mabel were coming along.' Emily's light tone belied the steely glint in her eyes and the Admiral blinked and looked over to his oldest friend whose face was going an interesting shade of grey.

'Charlie didn't think to mention that you were coming either,' offered Mabel in the same light-hearted manner while her eyes shot daggers at the Admiral.

The silence was anything but golden.

Then suddenly Emily's face changed as she looked over the Admiral's shoulder. 'I don't believe it', she breathed reverently before stepping towards Mabel and saying in a loud whisper. 'Don't look now Mabel but I think that's Darcy DeVine behind you.'

'No,' Mabel whispered back breathlessly, 'Is she with that producer - the one she ran off with?' Emily nodded with suppressed excitement. 'Blake Reynolds. And she's all over him like a rash, the shameless hussy.'

Of course, the Admiral didn't have quite the same respect for Hollywood royalty, given the fact that his son-in-law was one, and turned round, staring blatantly at the glittering couple heading towards them.

'What the bloody hell is she do…?' he started loudly. His question was fortunately cut short due to Mabel's not inconsiderable weight stomping down on his foot together with a glare that would stop a rampaging rhino in its tracks.

Emily tucked her arm in Mabel's, saying excitedly, 'What a story we'll have to tell at the Women's Institute next week. Let's see if they're with anyone else.' They wandered off, giggling like a pair of school girls, leaving the Admiral and Jimmy staring after them in bewilderment.

'I think a pint might be in order Jimmy lad,' murmured the Admiral after a minute, 'And while we're at the bar, you can tell me why the bloody hell you're dressed up as Al Capone's twin brother.'

As they headed into the bar, the Admiral realized that it wasn't just Jimmy and Emily who were dressed up, but the entire guest population looked as though they'd just stepped out of *The Great Gatsby*. All except him and Mabel.

'Pardon me for saying so Sir, but this is so typical of you,' Jimmy said, shaking his head in obvious irritation. 'You only ever bother to find out half the story before you go off half cocked.'

The Admiral looked at the small man in astonishment, but before he could say anything, Jimmy continued, 'We're at a murder mystery evening organized especially for Valentine's Day. They've called it *A Murderous Valentine*. It's supposed to be set in the roaring twenties. You didn't know that did you Sir? When you decided to bulldoze my romantic weekend with Emily, you had *no* idea what you were coming to. You just decided you were going to ruin everything and that was that.

'You Sir are probably *the* most selfish man I have *ever* met.' To the Admiral's amazement, his friend was actually shaking when he'd finished speaking.

Frowning Charles Shackleford opened his mouth to speak, but again Jimmy got there first, waving his finger under the Admiral's nose. 'Don't... just don't Sir, *don't* say anything. Now, what do you want to drink?'

The Admiral looked at the row of pumps on the bar. 'I'll have a pint of the local Jail Ale,' he responded soberly. 'Pretty bloody appropriate I'd say...'

By the time they'd been served, Mabel and Emily were firmly ensconced in some comfortable sofas tucked away in the corner, giving them a bird's eye view of the whole bar. Handing over two glasses of sherry, Jimmy turned to the Admiral and took his pint off him without speaking. Charles Shackleford sighed. He'd blundered badly and no mistake. He shook his head in bewilderment. It was so unlike him. Usually he was such a good judge of character.

Bit of a bloody turn up for the books – Jimmy growing backbone at this late stage. Still, he had to admit his former master at arms had given him cause for concern on a few occasions in recent months with the whole answering back thing – *and* actually making decisions without first consulting his commanding officer. The Admiral sighed. It would never have happened if he was still in charge. Morosely he stared around the bar.

Dozy DeWhateverhername was, was draping herself all over the producer chappy. He watched as the man turned towards him with a bored expression, completely ignoring his young companion. With a start, the Admiral realized that it was the same man he'd seen arguing in the corridor. He looked again at the actress. It certainly hadn't been with her. He glanced around, looking to see if the earlier woman was present, but there was no sign of her.

Frowning, he looked back towards the hotel entrance lobby, but that was deserted except for a lone man checking in. He was dressed in walking gear and carrying a backpack. Everything was liberally covered with rapidly melting snow. The Admiral winced and looked out of the window. The landscape was completely white. If this kept up, they wouldn't be going anywhere tomorrow.

Gradually he became aware that Emily was speaking. 'Apparently Darcy comes from these parts – just up the road in Tavistock I think. That's probably why they're here – visiting her family or something. Ooh, maybe they've got engaged. How thrilling. Do you think they'll announce it tonight?'

'Ooh I do hope so,' squeaked Mabel, squeezing her friend's arm excitedly. 'We'd definitely get the drop on old Agnes Dewbury if we came back with that little snippet.'

'Of course they're not going to announce their bollocking engagement,' interrupted the Admiral impatiently, 'If you ask me, she's up for the chop. He looks about as interested as an atheist at a vicar's tea party.'

They all looked over at the couple who were now surrounded by a large group of fawning admirers.

'It's just fashionable to look bored,' offered Emily knowledgeably, 'It doesn't mean anyth…'

'Rupert Montagu-Douglas-Smythe at your service.'

As one they turned to the newcomer who'd sneaked up unnoticed. Mabel and the Admiral looked perfectly baffled, but Jimmy and Emily had obviously done this before.

'Charmed I'm sure,' trilled Emily.

'Are you the owner of Wendleford Hall Sir?' questioned Jimmy self importantly, picking up a pad and pencil.

'I certainly am,' responded Rupert with an oily smile, 'And thank you all for coming to my eightieth birthday party.'

'What birthday party, and where's Wendleford bloody Hall?' the Admiral asked feeling as though he'd fallen down a rabbit hole.

'It's certainly a shock to find out you're stepping down as the head of your family business. It's all very sudden. Is there a reason for your decision Sir?' The Admiral looked over at Jimmy in astonishment.

'Alas, my health is becoming a concern and I'd like to spend what time I have left with my family…' He waved vaguely behind him.

'We'd certainly like to meet the rest of your family Mr. Montagu-Douglas-Smythe,' cut in Emily with a breathy little laugh.

'Rupert, dear lady. Please call me Rupert. You are my guests after all...'

'Okay *Rupert*,' the Admiral interrupted with a stern, 'I'll handle this,' look at his three companions, 'I don't know what bloody game you're playing but that oily tongue of yours won't cut the mustard with anyone of even the smallest intellectual capacity. I suggest you go and take a long walk off a short pier.'

Emily gasped, then gave a small titter. Jimmy glared at the Admiral before turning to look back at the now thunderous countenance of Mr. Rupert Montagu-Douglas-Smythe.

'Please don't mind my friend, *Rupert*, he's a little slow on the uptake and really doesn't get out much.' He ignored the Admiral's equally thunderous expression as he stood up to shake the man's hand. 'My wife and I are very much looking forward to the evening Sir.'

With a please don't mention it smile, Mr. Montagu-Douglas-Smythe bowed gracefully to the ladies and withdrew.

Turning to the Admiral, whose expression was warring between outrage and disbelief, Jimmy was briefly distracted by the novelty of his friend being lost for words. Of course it didn't last, but before the Admiral had chance to launch into a blistering tirade, Jimmy got there first.

'It's a murder mystery evening Sir. We're supposed to question all the possible suspects.'

The Admiral frowned. 'So who the bloody hell's been murdered?' he asked after a couple of seconds.

'Nobody – yet,' Jimmy answered patiently. 'The whole idea is that we get a feel for the cast so that we can guess who's done it after they actually do it.'

The Admiral narrowed his eyes. 'Well, it's nothing like that murder mystery shindig we had at Flo's house last year, but now I've got the hang of it, I'm sure we'll get to the bottom of whatever skullduggery they've cooked up.'

He turned to Mabel enthusiastically, 'Bit like Tommy and Tuppence Beresford, hey old girl?' All three simply looked back at him nonplussed, so he continued impatiently, 'You know, husband and wife sleuths, Agatha Christie and all that? If we pu…'

'Good evening, I'm Felicity Montagu-Douglas-Smythe. It's so nice to meet you.'

All eyes turned towards the stranger standing smiling behind them. Only she wasn't totally unfamiliar to the Admiral. With a start he recognised the woman who'd been arguing with the movie producer Blake Reynolds earlier.

# CHAPTER 4

To his irritation, the Admiral completely wasted the opportunity to question Miss Montagu-Douglas-Smythe or whatever her real name was.

They sat down for dinner in a foursome – Mabel and Emily had decided that conferring about Ditsy DeWhatswerface was more important than romance - but Charles Shackleford's mind was completely taken up by the unknown actress.

Had she been sporting a bruise on her cheek? Jimmy and Emily had asked a couple of useless questions, but he'd simply sat and stared at her until the other three had looked at him questioningly.

Now, at the table, they were still looking at him as though he'd suddenly sprouted two heads.

'Are you going to spit it out Sir?' Jimmy asked when the Admiral stared into space for the third time in as many minutes. 'The last time you were this quiet was when you'd arranged for old Bible Basher Boris to officiate at Tory's wedding without telling anybody.'

The Admiral frowned, wondering if he was making a mountain out of a mole hill. It wasn't often he questioned himself - especially given that he was generally always right – but now he felt an unaccustomed desire to share his concerns. It wouldn't hurt to get another perspective on the strange actions of the two guests earlier. Leaning forward, he quickly told the other three about his encounter in the corridor.

'So they obviously knew each other?' breathed Emily in excitement.

'No doubt about it,' Charles Shackleford answered. 'And what's more, I noticed a bruise on her cheek when she came over to us. Did that producer chappy give it to her? She certainly looked bloody scared when she was speaking to him. Determined, but definitely frightened.'

'Do you think one of us should go and speak to her?' Mabel interjected faintly.

Jimmy had had enough. 'This is ridiculous,' he sputtered, 'It's a *Murder Mystery evening*. How do you know that their meeting wasn't part of the whole set up? You can't just go over to the bloody woman, introduce yourself and say, By the way who gave you your black eye?'

'Yes we can,' the Admiral argued impatiently. 'It's exactly as you said Jimmy. We can act as though we think it's part of the evening's entertainment.'

'It probably is,' Jimmy reiterated a trifle sourly. The evening wasn't going how he'd planned it at all.

'So, who are those people sitting with Darcy and our suspect?' asked Emily, completely ignoring her husband's sulk.

'What exactly do we suspect him of?' Mabel responded curiously.

'Human trafficking?' speculated Emily darkly.

'Blackmail more likely,' offered the Admiral sagely, now in full Sherlock Holmes mode.

'But he's got bucket loads of money,' protested Jimmy. 'Why would he need to blackmail anybody?'

'Somebody could be blackmailing him,' Emily argued.

'Then he wouldn't be the bloody suspect would he?' Jimmy's sarcastic words elicited a narrow eyed look from his wife and he blanched slightly, subsiding into a brooding silence.

'Who's that gentleman sitting on the other side of Darcy?' questioned Mabel staring over at the large round table seating the actress, producer and six others.

As one they all turned to look.

'Don't make it obvious will you,' muttered Jimmy, glancing over despite himself.

'He looks as though he's going to be in her bloody lap any minute,' observed the Admiral.

'But she doesn't look happy about it does she?'

'Anyone recognize him?'

'He looks a bit like that chap off *Gardener's World*.'

'No, that's *Monty Don*. He doesn't look anything like *Monty Don*.'

'How about *Star Wars*?'

'How can you go from bloody *Gardener's World* to *Star Wars*?'

'Just thought he looked a bit like *Harrison Ford*.'

'*Harrison Ford* doesn't look a bit like *Monty Don*.'

'He's taken her arm. Look she's pulling away.'

'Would you like any bread Madam?'

Startled they all turned to look at the waiter who was regarding them politely.

'We need to formulate a plan,' said the Admiral sticking his hand in the basket.

'What the bloody hell do you call this?' he asked the waiter, eyeing the bread in his hand dubiously, 'And what are those black bits in it?'

'It's olive and oregano focaccia, Sir.'

'There's no need to swear,' said Mabel outraged.

The waiter went a crimson colour, sputtering, 'I didn't mean... I wasn't... it isn't... err, the bread's Italian Sir.'

'Ah.' The Admiral nodded sagely, 'That explains it.'

The waiter opened his mouth but couldn't think of an appropriate response to that little gem of wisdom. Instead, he simply plonked the basket of bread on the table and ran.

'We should get the opportunity to have a bit of a mingle and ask a few questions after we've finished the first course,' offered Emily, 'At least that's what normally happens. I suggest we split up and report back before the chicken.'

The other three nodded enthusiastically. Even Jimmy seemed to be getting the bug when he suggested they give themselves aliases, 'You know like in *Mission Impossible*...'

'Right,' said the Admiral after he'd finished his soup, 'I'll take the producer chappy. You take Dotty DeDoda, Emily. Jimmy, you interrogate that young sprig sitting next to her, and Mabel, you question Miss Montagu-Douglas-Smythe or whatever her name is.'

'Why can't I question Darcy?' queried Mabel petulantly.

'Because you're not as experienced in this sort of thing dear,' responded Emily patting her friend's hand kindly.

'What should I ask him?' queried Jimmy with a frown.

The Admiral sighed and rolled his eyes. 'You were a bloody Master At Arms, what's wrong with you? Have you had a brain fart Jimmy? Start by asking him his name and how he knows Da... Do... De... the bloody actress. Where does he live? Is he local, is he even English? Come on Jimmy, get your arse in gear.'

'I'm not really sure about this actually,' the small man responded, all thoughts of *Impossible Missions Force* disappearing quicker than you can say, *'Ethan Hunt.'*

'It's a long time since I questioned anyone at all. I might have been a service policeman, but that was a bloody long time ago.'

'You were *my* service policeman Jimmy and that should be enough. Just get on with it.' The Admiral looked over at the other guests who were beginning to move around and interact with the cast. 'Right then people we're on. Operation *Initial Intelligence* is a go.'

Shoving his chair back, he headed determinedly over to Blake Reynolds who had no idea what was about to hit him...

'Really Sir, I can't believe you actually asked him if he's done anyone in recently. He's a bloody guest. He can't possibly be our prospective murderer.'

'He looked damn shifty though – didn't you notice? Definitely got something to hide if you ask me. Look how he called over the manager pronto when I had him on the rack.'

'You nearly got thrown out Sir,' protested Jimmy in exasperation. 'He threatened to call his lawyer and sue you for slander.'

'I thought Darcy DeVine looked very tense over all the upset. I think she's hiding something,' Emily interjected thoughtfully. 'She was actually quite rude when I asked her about her forthcoming wedding. How about her friend, did you get anything out of him Jimmy?'

'As a matter of fact I did,' said Jimmy. 'He was quite chatty until

Charlie accused Blake Reynolds of plotting to murder Miss Montagu-Douglas-Sm...'

'Felicity,' interrupted Mabel. 'Can't you remember, she said her name was Felicity, but that's obviously not her real name. She flatly refused to admit she knew Blake Reynolds, and said she got that bruise from falling over in the shower.'

'Or was she pushed?' offered the Admiral thoughtfully, before turning back to Jimmy. 'So what did you get out of your suspect Jimmy boy?'

'His name is Ian Channing and he and Miss DeVine are old friends. Went to school together. Apparently they were childhood sweethearts – says he's never really gotten over her ditching him. Evidently she just upped and left Tavistock five years ago.'

'Oh how sad,' trilled Emily.

'Poor boy,' added Mabel.

'So what's he doing here tonight then?' the Admiral asked with a frown.

'Apparently Miss DeVine invited him. Maybe she felt a bit guilty for jilting him. Think our Mr. Channing might have been hoping for a re-run, but I get the feeling she put paid to that pretty sharpish.'

'So did Darcy actually leave Tavistock because she wanted to become an actress?' questioned Emily.

Jimmy puckered his brow. 'I'm not sure. Mr. Channing didn't actually say why she left. In fact I got the impression that Miss DeVine didn't head for the bright lights immediately after they split. I think it was a few months later. She just suddenly disappeared one day.'

'HOW COULD YOU DO THIS FATHER?' The shout nearly had the four of them jumping out of their seats.

'HOW COULD YOU CHOOSE BERTIE AS YOUR SUCCESSOR TO

THE FAMILY BUSINESS INSTEAD OF ME? IS IT BECAUSE I'M A WOMAN?'

The Admiral had to admit Miss Montagu-Douglas-Smythe was a bloody good actress. She certainly threw herself into her role.

'SEE THIS BRUISE ON MY CHEEK? WHO DO YOU THINK DID THAT FATHER? IT WAS BERTIE. HE PUSHED ME DOWN THE STAIRS. THAT'S THE KIND OF MAN HE IS.'

Jimmy turned and smirked at the Admiral at this little revelation, but Charles Shackleford didn't notice. He narrowed his eyes. He could smell improvisation a mile off – after all, it was his stock in trade. Felicity Montagu-Douglas-Smythe had just ad-libbed that little bit of information in.

'FOR GOD'S SAKE FELICITY CALM YOURSELF.' An older woman previously unnoticed by the Admiral entered the fray.

'HOW CAN YOU SAY THAT MOTHER? HOW CAN YOU ALLOW FATHER TO DO THIS TO ME?'

'DO YOU THINK YOUR MOTHER HAS ANY SAY OVER MY BUSINESS DECISIONS FELICITY? SHE DOESN'T CARE – THE ONLY THING SHE CARES ABOUT IS HER AFFAIR WITH MY BROTHER ARCHIE.'

'AND WHAT ABOUT YOUR AFFAIR RUPERT? DO YOU THINK I DIDN'T KNOW ABOUT YOUR SORDID LITTLE TRYSTS WITH THE MAID?'

The whole cast gasped… and then the chicken was brought in and everyone clapped.

'See,' offered Jimmy smugly, 'No mention of Blake Reynolds. I'm afraid you're way off the mark Sir. Like I told you, the producer's a guest like us.'

The Admiral didn't answer immediately. He stared over at the cast where there appeared to be a whispered argument going on.

'Young Felicity stuck that bit in about her bruise without consulting the rest of the cast, and they're not best happy about it.' He nodded towards the actors. 'That means whatever happened to her had nothing to do with the murder mystery.'

Jimmy looked over at Felicity. She certainly appeared upset and the rest of the cast looked thunderous. 'I think you might be right Sir,' he mused thoughtfully as the actors trooped out of the room for a break. 'So maybe Blake Reynolds did give her that bruise after all. But the question is, why?'

# CHAPTER 5

The Admiral looked at his watch. 'How long have we got until the next act?' he asked.' I could do with another pint and a visit to the heads. How about you Jimmy lad?'

They'd eaten the main course without any further speculation. Emily made it clear that all talk of murder should be suspended while she was eating – she said it made her bilious.

'I wouldn't mind another one Sir, while you're up at the bar.'

The Admiral got to his laboriously to his feet, saying 'How about you two ladies, fancy another tipple?'

'I say Emily,' said Mabel, clutching her friend's arm enthusiastically, 'Shall we be naughty and have one of those Piss Echoes?'

'What the bloody hell's a Piss Echo?' asked the Admiral absently. He'd noticed Dooby DeDowhat leaving the dining room with her ex, Ian Channing.

'Ooh yes,' agreed Emily, 'I had one of those at Tory's wedding. Went straight to my head.' She giggled and Jimmy went very pink. 'Shall we have a bottle?'

'You can have a bloody crate if you want,' answered the Admiral, straining to see where the actress had gone.

'There's no need to be rude Charlie,' retorted Emily, but she was speaking to the large man's back. The Admiral was hurrying towards the bar in an effort to catch up with the couple. Unfortunately, by the time he got out of the dining room, the pair had vanished.

Frowning, he had a look round, but there was no sign of them at the bar or cozying up in any corners. Perhaps they were having a bit of assignation out in the lobby.

Determined not to let the opportunity slip, he decided to have a quick look before he paid a visit to the heads. However the large entrance hall was deserted. Even the reception desk was unoccupied.

The Admiral stopped and looked around. The only noise came from a roaring fire crackling in the huge fireplace. There were a couple of cosy alcoves sporting comfortable sofas under the windows but a quick check confirmed that both were unoccupied. Glancing out of the window, the Admiral could hardly see anything at all. The snow had stopped but the clouds remained, indicating the possibility of more to come before the night was over.

Shaking his head, the Admiral decided that for the moment his other needs were becoming slightly more pressing and without further ado, he forced himself to put aside his detective hat and hastened to the gents.

'I've never been so bloody embarrassed Mabel. The barman laughed his head off when I asked for a Piss Echo. Apparently it's called Prows Echo. More dodgy Italian imports. Looks like bloody Babycham to me.' The Admiral put his tray down and glanced over at Blake Reynolds. To his surprise, Ian Channing had returned but there was no sign of his companion.

'When did Mr Jilted arrive back? he asked, handing Jimmy his pint. Jimmy looked over at their table in surprise. 'I didn't realize he'd left.'

'Bollocking hell Jimmy, get a grip. You're behaving like a lost fart in a haunted milk bottle.'

Jimmy reddened and opened his mouth to retaliate, but before he could get a word out, there was a kerfuffle in the far corner and the cast were on again.

'TAKE THAT YOU BLAGGARD.'

'Ouch,' murmured Emily wincing, 'That looked painful.'

'Old Rupert's got a damn good right hook,' added Jimmy, 'He looked as though he really clobbered that chap – what's his name - Archie is it?'

'His brother,' offered Mabel helpfully.

'I WILL NOT ALLOW YOU TO HAVE MY WIFE. SHE'S THE ONLY THING I HAVE LEFT. I'LL NEVER SET HER FREE.'

'BUT WHAT ABOUT ME FATHER. YOU HAVE ME.' Felicity fell to the floor at her father's feet sobbing theatrically.

'WHAT GOOD ARE YOU TO ME IF YOU REFUSE TO MARRY BERTIE,' her father thundered, before turning to his wife. 'THE MAID MEANT NOTHING TO ME MARGARET, NOTHING.'

'I'M YOUR ELDEST CHILD,' cried Felicity. 'SURELY I'M MORE TO YOU THAN MARRIAGE FODDER?'

'YOU'RE A WOMAN FELICITY,' snapped Bertie, taking her arm and pulling her roughly to her feet. 'YOU NEED A MAN TO TAKE YOU IN HAND.'

'IT'S NO GOOD RUPERT, I DON'T LOVE YOU ANYMORE. ARCHIE AND I ARE LEAVING.'

'IF YOU LEAVE THIS HOUSE, I WILL CUT YOU OUT OF MY WILL MARGARET. YOU MIGHT BE TWENTY YEARS YOUNGER THAN ME, BUT YOU WON'T SEE A PENNY.'

'I DON'T CARE. MY HEART BELONGS TO ARCHIE.' The lovelorn Margaret picked her unfortunate lover off the floor.

He really did look as if he'd been thumped reflected the Admiral, it was a good job he only had a bit part.

'I'M LEAVING YOU RUPERT AND THERE'S NOTHING YOU CAN DO TO STOP ME.'

'MOTHER, PLEASE DON'T GO,' implored Felicity, raising her arm. For a second Margaret turned towards her daughter before deliberately turning her back and helping Archie out of the room.

'NOOOOOO,' screamed Felicity in anguish, tearing at her hair and throwing herself at Bertie who staggered under her onslaught. There was a slight hush as the second act came to an end, followed by a thunderous applause.

Emily shook her head, wiping away a tear. 'That young woman should be on the Big Screen. That was an Oscar winning performance.'

Blinking, the Admiral nodded before suddenly noticing that Blake Reynolds was walking away from his table.

'Where's Darcy?' asked Mabel abruptly noticing the actress's absence.

'She went off with that Channing chap before the second act started,' the Admiral commented. 'I had a look for them while I was out, but I didn't see where they went.' He nodded towards Ian Channing, 'Mr Lovesick was back at the table when I got back with the drinks, but I've no idea where Miss Hollywood has got to.' He paused, indicating Blake Reynolds disappearing back. 'And I wonder where our producer's off to now.'

'Maybe he's gone to look for her,' speculated Jimmy.

'Ooh Cream Bullet,' interrupted Mabel as the waiter approached their table. 'My favourite.'

'There's got to be a bloody murder soon,' muttered the Admiral as he tucked into his dessert. 'I'm beginning to get a bollocking headache with all this thinking. Is it hot in here?' Charles Shackleford pulled at his jacket and mopped his forehead with his napkin as Jimmy looked over at him in alarm.

'Perhaps you're overdoing it Sir. I mean it's only been a few months since your heart attack. Maybe all this thinking is too much for you.' The Admiral gave his friend a withering glance.

'Using my noggin is unlikely to see me pushing up daisies Jimmy. I've just got overheated that's all. As soon as I've finished this, I'll take a little turn outside.'

'But Charlie, you can't go outside,' protested Mabel worriedly, 'Look at the weather.'

'Don't worry old girl,' the Admiral grunted dipping a piece of shortbread into his Crème Brulee, 'I'll just stand in the porch.'

Looking back over at Blake Reynolds' table, the Admiral saw the producer seating himself back with his guests. The actress's chair was still conspicuously empty and Charles Shackleford felt his earlier sense of unease come flooding back. Either something nasty was about to happen, or he'd eaten too much of that bloody Italian bread...

Belching discreetly so as not to offend the ladies, he got to his feet. 'I'll come with you Sir,' offered Jimmy pushing his chair back, 'I could do with a bit of fresh air myself.' He turned back to Mabel and Emily. 'We won't be long ladies, I'll get you both another bottle of Prows Echo on my way back,' he offered, winking at Emily who blushed in response.

With that he hurried after the Admiral in the direction of the bar.

'Perhaps Miss DeVine felt unwell and decided to retire early,' mused the small man, catching the Admiral up just as they passed the actress's still empty chair. The Admiral frowned. 'She didn't look unwell when she wandered off with that Channing chappy. And anyway, if she was going to call it a day, why didn't she tell anyone?'

'She might have done,' responded Jimmy as they crossed the bar. 'Blake Reynolds could have been up to check on her when he left his table.'

Charles Shackleford nodded thoughtfully. 'I'm beginning to think you're right Jimmy lad, he said as they got to the entrance hall, 'I really think I'm too bloody clever for my own good. I'll be identifying half a dozen murders if I keep going at this rate and nobody's actually been done in yet.' The two men chuckled.

'I'm just going to make a quick stop at the heads,' Jimmy decided as they made their way to the hotel entrance, 'I'll see you outside in a couple of minutes Sir.' The Admiral waved his hand in acknowledgement before hunching down in his jacket and stepping outside.

The night was absolutely bitter. Charles Shackleford stamped his feet and blew on his hands. It was cold enough to freeze the balls off a brass monkey. He wouldn't be staying out for long.

An eerie silence enveloped the frozen landscape, the snow muffling any sound like a large white blanket. The Admiral looked up, just as the clouds parted to reveal a bright moon, almost full, turning the scene to liquid silver.

Glancing round in awe, he suddenly noticed a bench about twenty yards away. He stared at it for a second wondering why it looked so odd, then he frowned in realisation - for some reason it was clear of snow. His eyes travelled to the left of the seat. On the ground was a small shadowed mound.

He looked down at the two sets of footprints leading towards the bench. Heart pounding he followed their tracks until he was standing next to the thing on the ground. Only it wasn't a thing. Taking one last step, he found himself looking into the empty eyes of Darcy DeVine.

# CHAPTER 6

The dark stain decorating the front of Darcy's sequined gown proclaimed this was no accident. The Admiral stood rooted to the spot for a few seconds, then glanced around wildly. Whoever had done it could still be in the vicinity. There were no tracks leading away from the body to indicate that someone had fled the scene.

Panicked, he backed away from the still form of the actress as the moon again disappeared behind the clouds. Then a few seconds later he was running. The twenty yards to the front door of the hotel felt like a hundred, and every step of the way, he expected to feel the blade of a knife in his back.

Staggering into the welcoming warmth of the hotel, he ran into Jimmy who was coming out to meet him. For a few seconds he was almost incoherent until the small man, using a tone the Admiral hadn't heard in years, commanded him to stop and start again from the beginning.

'There's a body. On the ground outside. It's the actress.' Charles Shackleford shook his head to shut out the sight of Darcy DeVine's lifeless eyes. 'She's dead Jimmy,' he whispered finally. 'She's really dead. What are we going to do?'

Jimmy stared into the frightened face of his oldest friend. The sight of a terrified Charles Shackleford was so incongruous that for a couple of seconds he expected him to suddenly start laughing, proclaiming the whole thing a huge joke. Then from nowhere, his master at arms training kicked in. He knew how to secure a crime scene. It had been his job for over ten years.

'Go and inform the management,' he told the Admiral in a voice that brooked no argument. 'Tell them there's been an incident, then call the police.' He glanced towards the still open door, 'Though God knows how they're going to actually get here in this weather.'

He turned back to the Admiral who hadn't moved. 'Under no circumstances is anyone to come outside Sir, do you understand? They could well destroy valuable evidence.' He gave the large man a little push, then headed outside, closing the door firmly behind him.

The Admiral shut his eyes for a second and took a few deep breaths feeling completely ashamed. There was no doubt about it, he'd gone to pieces out there. He needed to pull himself together, behave like a man in charge.

Straightening his jacket he looked over at the reception desk which was still deserted. Where the bloody hell was everyone? He glanced down at his watch and was startled to see that it was already past ten pm. The receptionist at the desk earlier was most likely off duty by now.

Making a decision, he hurried through to the bar and was just about to ask the bar man to find him someone in charge, when he heard a loud cry from the dining room.

'OH MY GOD SHE'S DEAD.'

'Bollocks,' the Admiral muttered. Had someone got to the body before him? Determinedly he strode over to the dining room, pausing briefly in the doorway before shouting, 'NOBODY LEAVE THIS ROOM.'

All eyes turned to him and it had to be said he got a little carried away by the drama of the situation.

'WHO FOUND THE BODY?' he bellowed to the astonishment of the entire dining room. There was a pause, then a confused, 'Err, I did.'

The Admiral glared at the owner of the voice. 'WAS SHE LYING NEXT TO THE BENCH?'

Another pause. 'Err, no she was lying in her bedroom.'

'SO YOU ADMIT YOU MOVED THE BODY.' The Admiral was on a roll now and pointed his finger accusingly at the speaker who he finally registered was a member of the cast. What was his name? Bob... Billy... Brian... damn it.

'WHAT'S YOUR NAME SIR?' he asked striding towards the bewildered man who was looking behind him in panic.

'Bertie?' the man offered uncertainly after a couple of seconds

'WHAT ARE YOU TALKING ABOUT?' Rupert Montagu-Douglas-Smythe, who was clearly the lead actor, took charge and stepped past the unfortunate Bertie. 'FELICITY WAS FOUND IN HER BEDROOM.'

'FELICITY'S DEAD?' The Admiral was flabbergasted. Two murders in as many minutes. He needed to contact the authorities as soon as possible.

'NO... YES... IT'S A BLOODY MURDER MYSTERY YOU IDIOT. SIT DOWN FOR GOD'S SAKE, YOU'RE RUINING OUR PERFORMANCE.'

It suddenly dawned on the Admiral that he'd walked in just as they were announcing the fictional murder. Felicity wasn't really dead after all. He breathed a sigh of relief before snapping back to the present and facing the rest of the cast who were regarding him with various expressions ranging from outright fury to mild irritation. Straightening up, he puffed out his chest and addressed the whole room solemnly.

'A BODY HAS BEEN FOUND OUTSIDE. I AM ABOUT TO NOTIFY THE POLICE. PLEASE REMAIN IN THIS ROOM UNTIL YOU ARE TOLD OTHERWISE.' Then turning on his heel, he asked the startled barman to find him a phone.

Jimmy crouched down and stared at the corpse. It was hard to believe she'd once been vibrant and alive. Now she looked almost as if she'd been made of wax. An exhibit at Madame Tussaud's perhaps.

Without touching the body, he peered down at the wound. The blood had pooled in her stomach cavity and then frozen due to the extreme temperatures. Taking a deep breath he rocked back on his heels. There was no doubt this was murder, and off the top of his head, he would guess it had been done by an extremely sharp knife.

Resisting the temptation to look around for the murder weapon, he stood up gingerly, knowing it was vital he didn't compromise the crime scene any more than it was already. Turning round, he walked slowly back to the hotel entrance taking care to step in the tracks he'd made previously. Before entering, he glanced up at the sky. If it snowed again now, all evidence might well be lost within half an hour.

Grimly, he strode into the lobby and spied the Admiral on the phone. The night manager stood next to him white faced.

Jimmy hurried over to the desk. 'Do you have keys to all the bedrooms in the hotel Ken?' he asked the man sombrely, after reading the manager's name on the badge pinned to his chest. Ken nodded tensely and turned round to unhook a large bunch of keys.

'Would you be so kind as to knock on each bedroom door and request any inhabitants to vacate their rooms as soon as possible and assemble in the dining room?' continued Jimmy. 'If no-one answers, it's important you verify the room is empty. Could you also check all the public areas including the cloakrooms? Once all the guests are assembled, please ask all members of staff and actors to do the same. Do you have a list of guests currently at the hotel?' Again Ken nodded.

'Once you think everyone staying in the hotel has been gathered together, could you please inform me?' Jimmy waited, expecting to meet some resistance; however Ken didn't argue, but simply hastened towards the stairs.

Putting the phone down, the Admiral turned to Jimmy. 'The police are on their way,' he said soberly.

Jimmy sagged visibly before saying tiredly, 'The most important thing is to ensure the primary crime scene remains untouched.' Charles Shackleford nodded, eyeing the small man critically. He hadn't seen this side to Jimmy Noon since they were both in uniform.

'I'll wait by the phone,' Jimmy was saying, 'Perhaps you could go back into the dining room and reassure Emily and Mabel. They must be worried sick by now.'

Unaccustomed to being given orders, the Admiral was about to argue, when he spied the fear in his friend's eyes. It was easy to forget that in all probability they had a murderer in their midst.

'Please make sure that no-one leaves the room Sir, and say as little as you can about what's happened,' Jimmy added as if reading his mind.

It was going to be a long night.

## CHAPTER 7

As the Admiral entered the dining room, everyone started clamouring to find out exactly what had happened. Shutting the door behind him, Charles Shackleford put up his hands to the crowd jostling him.

'ALL I CAN TELL YOU IS THAT THERE HAS BEEN AN INCIDENT,' he bellowed, 'THE POLICE ARE ON THEIR WAY, AND IN THE MEANTIME HAVE REQUESTED THAT WE ALL REMAIN IN THIS ROOM FOR OUR OWN SAFETY.'

There was a brief silence in the wake of his announcement, then everyone started speaking at once. The Admiral pushed through the throng until he finally managed to reach Mabel and Emily.

'What a bloody cake and arse party,' he muttered as he sat down gratefully.

Contrary to Jimmy's prediction both ladies were eager to hear what had happened. The Admiral took a long draft of his pint then leant forward conspiratorially.

'Is it Darcy?' Emily asked before he got chance to speak.

A bit miffed that she'd pre-empted his thunder, the Admiral frowned, then nodded reluctantly. Both ladies shook their heads sadly as he continued, 'Jimmy's waiting for the police. I can't say much more, but it's a bloody rum do and no mistake.'

An arm grabbed the Admiral's shoulder roughly. 'Did I hear you mention Darcy's name?' Turning, Charles Shackleford came face to face with a wild-eyed Ian Channing. Behind him stood Blake Reynolds, his expression giving nothing away.

The Admiral sighed. 'You heard right,' he said sternly. 'The body is Darcy DeVine's, but that's all I know.'

'Was… was she murdered?' the young man whispered, horror and grief vying for supremacy in his voice.

'I'm afraid I can't say,' the Admiral responded carefully, for once managing to follow instructions.

'Can't or won't?' asked Blake Reynolds evenly.

'If she was murdered,' went on Ian Channing loudly, 'Then that means someone in this room could be the one who did it.' He looked around wildly. 'We could be sharing this room with a killer.'

The silence was so complete you could have heard a pin drop. Everyone stared at the person next to them with fear and suspicion. The Admiral got to his feet. He knew the next stage was panic. If he wasn't careful, he and Jimmy could end up with a bloody stampede on their hands.

Glancing over to the door, he saw various members of staff being ushered in by Ken, the night manager. Standing on his own to one side was the lone walker he'd seen check in earlier in the evening. The man had clearly dressed hurriedly and looked completely bewildered by the whole situation. The Admiral couldn't help but feel sorry for him. It was obvious he'd been asleep.

Abandoning the Admiral's table, the crowd suddenly came back to life and surged towards the hapless manager who for a second looked as though he was going to go down in the onslaught. However, he bravely stood his ground and refused to let anyone go through the door. With a muttered oath, the Admiral told Emily and Mabel to stay put and pushed through to give the manager some support.

'PLEASE RETURN TO YOUR TABLES,' the night manager shouted. 'THE POLICE WILL BE HERE SHORTLY. IN THE MEANTIME, A MEMBER OF STAFF WILL BRING COFFEE TO THOSE WHO WANT IT.'

'Never mind a coffee,' ventured a lone voice, 'A bloody brandy would be more like it.' Luckily the dry remark effectively dashed cold water on the rising emotions spreading around the room, and a few people even cheered.

Releasing a breath he didn't know he'd been holding, the Admiral asked Ken if he was alright. The man nodded bleakly before instructing the waiting staff to operate the coffee machine standing in the corner.

As the guests began trickling back to their tables, the dining room door suddenly opened. It was a grim faced Jimmy.

'How long before the police get here? asked the Admiral, anxious to hand over the reins to somebody else. Jimmy shook his head slowly.

'They're not coming Sir. The weather's closing in and it's too dangerous to bring out the snow ploughs until morning.' He paused and eyed the Admiral unhappily. 'Until then I'm afraid it's just us. When I told them I was a service policeman, they instructed me to start the investigation into Darcy DeVine's murder and process the crime scene before the weather totally obliterates any clues the killer might have left.'

The small man took a deep breath. 'I'm going to need your help Sir because nobody else is allowed to leave the hotel.'

## CHAPTER 8

The Admiral headed back up to their room to grab his coat. He wasn't about to freeze his bollocks off standing around in the sub zero temperatures.

As he entered, Pickles lifted his head slightly before sighing loudly and settling back down into the quilt. 'Don't think you're staying there all night you sorry hound,' the Admiral muttered giving the dog a quick fuss, 'As soon as we've got this body thing sorted, you'll be out there freezing your knackers off too.'

He hurried back down to the entrance hall where Jimmy was waiting, already wrapped up and armed with a torch, a large sheet of tarpaulin and a notebook and pen. The small man handed the Admiral the pen and paper. 'If it's all the same with you Sir, I'd like you to stand well back and take notes.' The Admiral nodded.

'What would you like me to do?' asked Ken as they turned to walk outside.

'Could you tick off the names on your guest list and make sure that everyone is present in the dining room?' Jimmy requested. Ken gave the thumbs up and hurried back to the dining room.

As they stepped out of the porch, Jimmy rummaged in his pocket for a pair of rubber gloves he'd taken from the hotel's first aid kit and gave an anxious look towards the starless sky. 'We need to get a move on Sir, I think it could start snowing again any moment.'

After instructing the Admiral to stand in the first set of the footprints he'd made earlier, Jimmy put the tarpaulin onto the ground and carefully placed his feet into his own prints. Then he bent down with his torch and painstakingly examined the two sets of footprints that hadn't been made by him or the Admiral.

'We've got a bit of a print,' he commented, 'But probably not enough to identify the assailant's footwear. The snow is quite impacted so I'd guess our suspect was probably wearing boots. That, together with the size of the print indicates it was most likely a man.' The Admiral didn't answer, but scribbled down everything Jimmy was saying. 'The other set is definitely a woman's. The sole and the heel correspond with the type of shoes Miss DeVine was wearing.'

Directing his torch onto the ground, Jimmy took half a dozen photos with his mobile phone. Then straightening up, he stared towards the corpse.

'The only footprints that appear to be heading back towards the hotel entrance are yours and mine, so the killer didn't return this way.'

Cautiously the small man made his way towards the body before stopping a couple of feet away. Slowly swinging his torch in an arc, he painstakingly examined the bushes that were growing in an ornamental half circle about a foot from where Darcy DeVine's head had its final resting place.

'The snow hasn't been dislodged from any of the bushes here,' he commented, before crouching down again to examine the snow on either side of the body, 'And the snow on either side of her is untouched except from the footprints you and I made.'

He shone his torch towards the bench and pointed. 'The other two sets of prints head directly to the seat and you can see where the snow has been trampled. That's where any scuffle, if there was one, took place. But my guess is the murderer caught her unawares as they sat on the bench.'

Standing, he took more photos of the area around the body, then taking a deep breath, stepped closer to the corpse and hunkered back down. For a while he said nothing, simply panned the light of his torch across her torso.

'There don't appear to be any obvious wounds on her body apart from what seems to be a single knife wound to her chest. The lack of disturbance around the corpse indicates she likely fell backwards as she was stabbed.' He leaned forward. 'She didn't bleed out as much as she would have done in normal circumstances...'

'You think anything about this bollocking load of horlicks is normal?' interrupted the Admiral loudly, trying to lighten the mood slightly.

Jimmy turned his head and smiled slightly, gratefully, before turning back to the body. 'The cold obviously sealed the wound fairly quickly. In fact, had our man stabbed her a little bit to the right, the cold might have saved her life.' He sighed again. 'The knife wound looks to be directly into her heart, although we won't know for sure until an autopsy is performed. I'm not sure if it was a lucky strike or whether the assailant has some specialist anatomical knowledge.'

Placing his knees carefully into the snow, Jimmy leant forward towards the actress's head. Shining the torch into her face, he shook his head sadly. 'Such a beautiful young woman,' he murmured to himself.

'There doesn't appear to be any bruising on her face,' he called back to the Admiral. Then moving his torch down her right arm, he noticed some livid marks above her elbow. Frowning he lifted the arm to confirm the marks went right round, then panned the torch over her other arm. Nothing.

'I think our killer is right handed. There are finger marks on her upper right arm but none on her left. In all likelihood, he gripped her arm with his left hand to hold her still, before stabbing her with his right.'

Jimmy shone the torch back to her head and gingerly pushed it to one side. The ground was sticky underneath and the hair matted at the back of her head. 'She fell pretty heavily, hitting her head on the concrete. I think the killer had to have stabbed her with a lot of force for her to have gone down as hard as she did. Maybe our suspect was angry, or possibly jealous?'

Placing the torch on the ground, Jimmy held the head in position and photographed the wound together with the ground underneath. Then directing his torch back onto her arms, he photographed the marks on her right arm and the lack of them on her left. Finally, he took some shots of the stab wound before straightening up and taking several of the whole body.

Stepping carefully to the right, he went on to examine the bench. 'The snow's been brushed off, and not with half measures either. I think whoever brought Darcy out here cleaned the bench beforehand, which indicates the murder could well have been premeditated.' He glanced back at the body. 'She's not wearing any coat, so she didn't expect to be out here long, but everything points to the fact that she knew her attacker.'

Jimmy shone the torch on the ground around the bench. 'But how did our man flee the scene?' he muttered. Frowning, he panned the torch back onto the seat itself and bent closer. 'There's a footprint on the wooden slats,' he said excitedly, 'And another on the top of the bench.' He shone his torch upwards. 'The snow's been dislodged on this drain pipe and on that window sill.' He pointed his torch up at a small window next to the downpipe. 'I think our assailant climbed up and went through that window.'

After quickly taking the required photographic evidence, Jimmy finally turned and made his way back to where the Admiral was shivering and stamping his feet.

'Not long now Sir,' he said, bending down to pick up the tarpaulin, 'I just need to cover the body, then we'll be heading back inside.'

'Thank God for that,' the Admiral groaned, 'I don't mind telling you, my knackers are solid ice right now…'

## CHAPTER 9

After quickly divesting themselves of their outdoor gear, Jimmy and the Admiral headed towards the stairs, intending to track down the window that may have provided the murderer with his escape route.

It took them about fifteen minutes to finally discover the right one at the end of a narrow service corridor on the first floor. Jimmy examined the window closely and pointed at the loose paint on the sill.

'See that Sir,' he said, 'This window hasn't been opened for a bloody long time. Our man had to force it which dislodged some of the paint. He wouldn't have been able to do that hanging on to a drainpipe, so he had to have planned it beforehand.' He bent closer to the sill as the Admiral furiously scribbled down his friend's observations.

'There's a partial boot print here – it looks like the back of a heel. His boots took off a bit more of the paint when he jumped down.' Jimmy pointed to the white flakes on the carpet before backing along the corridor, staring at the floor. After six feet or so, he shook his head. 'Here's where the boot prints end unfortunately, so I don't think we're going to have much luck discovering where the killer went after he climbed through the window.'

He walked back towards the Admiral and looked again at the window frame. 'Given what we know about our killer, I don't think he's likely to have been stupid enough to leave any finger prints, but we'd better check anyway.

'Sir, could I ask you to pop down to the kitchen to see if you can find some cocoa powder, sellotape and a dry pastry brush?'

The Admiral had taken more orders from his former Master At Arms in the last hour than he had in forty years. It went totally against the grain, but reluctantly impressed by his old friend's forensic skills, he swallowed a caustic retort and reluctantly headed down to the kitchen.

It took him over ten minutes to locate the kitchen which turned out to be a cavernous room with a sea of stainless steel. Charles Shackleford stared round in dismay. It would take him a couple of hours to locate some bloody cocoa and probably even longer to dig out some bollocking sellotape. And what in God's name was a damn pastry brush?

Sighing, he started opening cupboard doors. At this rate the bloody murderer will have booked and gone on his holidays by the time they managed to get any finger prints. Yanking open a large drawer, he saw a small brush with a wooden handle. 'Bingo - that's got to be it,' he thought, holding it up.

One down, two to go. Now where the bloody hell would they keep the cocoa? Glancing over the other side of the room, he noticed a row of large tins set behind a block of knives. Heartened, he hurried over, pushed aside the block and poked his head inside the tins. To his delight, the third one held a brown powdery substance. 'That'll do,' he muttered, picking up the tin.

After opening a few more drawers in a futile search for sellotape, he had a sudden brainwave and clutching his booty, he headed out of the kitchen and made his way to the reception desk.

Two minutes later he was climbing the stairs triumphantly with all the items Jimmy had asked for.

'This is gravy powder,' Jimmy declared when he looked down at the contents of the tin. 'Didn't you think to smell it Sir?' The Admiral sighed. Things were not looking up. Jimmy was beginning to get ideas above his station.

'It's brown and it's powder, stop bloody winging and just get on with it Sherlock,' he answered irritably.

There weren't any fingerprints as Jimmy had suspected. There was however a strong smell of roast beef.

Frustrated, Jimmy opened the window and leaned out. It had finally started snowing again.

'Could you help me up onto the sill Sir?' he asked, turning back to the Admiral. Charles Shackleford sighed. He'd bloody well had enough of playing detective.

Bending down, he boosted his friend onto the window sill and watched as Jimmy leaned precariously out into the night. 'I think we might be able to get something from the drainpipe,' the small man said excitedly a few seconds later. 'There's something caught on a nail.' He stuck his head back in. 'Right Sir, you grab my legs and lower me down slowly. I'll tell you when I'm in the right position.'

With that, Jimmy turned to lie across the sill, his head outside and his feet sticking back inside like a geriatric trapeze artist. Tetchily, the Admiral grabbed hold of his friend's legs and shoved a little more forcefully than perhaps was necessary.

'Bloody heeeell,' yelled Jimmy as he suddenly shot out of the window executing a first class swallow dive followed by a dull thud as he hit the drain pipe.

'Bugger,' grunted the Admiral who only just managed to prevent the small man from landing head first next to the corpse, and was now having a great deal of difficulty hanging onto Jimmy's legs – especially as his trousers were not the best fit. 'What the bloody hell did you have to wear someone else's bollocking pegs for?' he muttered, trying to get a better grip as Jimmy's trousers slowly began to slide over his hips.

'PULL ME UP, PULL ME UP,' Jimmy yelled waving the scrap of whatever it was in the air.

'Easier said than done,' huffed the Admiral as the small man's trousers slowly slid towards his knees.

Knowing that in a few seconds Jimmy was likely to be hitting the bench below with his dignity round his ankles, the Admiral took a chance. It was all or nothing. Letting go of one leg he lunged forward to grab the back of his friend's jacket and yanked.

There was an ominous ripping sound, then Jimmy came hurtling backwards through the window, only narrowly missing shoving the Admiral's chin up his nostrils. The force of his re-entry sent them both flying through the air to land in a heap six feet away.

Panting, the two men lay on the floor. Thankfully neither appeared to have anything broken, although Jimmy's jacket sported a large tear across the back. 'That's going to cost me,' he moaned sitting up gingerly.

'Never mind your bloody jacket,' the Admiral grumbled, 'What about my bollocking back? Have you put weight on?'

Jimmy didn't answer, but instead held up the small scrap of cloth he'd prised from the drainpipe. 'Do you think it belongs to the murderer?' the Admiral asked sitting up.

'No idea,' Jimmy responded, 'But it's a clue that might be useful to the plods when they finally pole up tomorrow.'

'Don't you worry Jimmy lad,' the Admiral said, clambering stiffly to his feet, 'At the rate we're going we'll have solved the murder and be down in time for breakfast. So, what's next?'

'Next?' Jimmy repeated thoughtfully, 'First, I change my jacket, and then we start asking questions…'

# CHAPTER 10

When the two men entered the dining room ten minutes later, Ken looked very relieved to see them.

'Is everyone here?' asked Jimmy glancing around at the sombre faces of the guests and staff. Ken nodded.

'What about the cast from the Theatre Company. Where are they?'

'In the snug,' responded Ken, pointing to a small room Jimmy hadn't noticed before. He realized this was where the cast had appeared from at the start of each act.

'We need to start asking people questions Ken,' the small man continued. 'We haven't got an exact time of death but we know Darcy DeVine left the room at approximately nine fifteen and Admiral Shackleford discovered the body at just after ten pm. So, first things first, we have to eliminate those people who never left this room during that time period.' Jimmy took the guest list from the manager and glanced down at it. 'Is this accurate?' he asked after a moment.

'Yes, everyone on the list is in this room, with the addition of Mr. Jackson who was a walk-in this evening.'

Jimmy looked up. 'And as well as the guests, there are nine members of staff including yourself, and five members of the err... Murder She Spoke Theatre Company?' Ken simply nodded.

'Right then,' Jimmy said decisively, 'Can you make two more copies of this list and add the names of all your staff. Once you've done that, we'll split the room into three. Admiral Shackleford and I will take the guests and the cast, while you question your staff. Happy Ken?'

The night manager looked anything but happy, but all he said was, 'What kind of questions should I ask them?'

'We simply want to know where each person was between nine fifteen and ten pm, and whether they were alone, or with someone. If they were with someone, make sure you get that someone's name. It's important you find out each member of staff's movements during the *whole* of that period.'

As Ken hurried off, Jimmy turned to the Admiral who'd been uncharacteristically quiet. There was a gleam in the large man's eyes that Jimmy had seen all too often and the familiar alarm bells started ringing insistently.

'Remember Sir, these are just preliminary questions,' he said urgently. 'We're not going to be making any accusations. If we come up with anything concrete, we'll leave the police to make an arrest when they arrive tomorrow.'

The Admiral's nodded his head in restrained excitement, saying, 'Absolutely Jimmy lad. Asking questions is what I'm good at. We'll get to the bottom of this business and we'll hand the blaggard over to the plod with a bow on when they get here. Operation *Murderous Valentine* is a go.'

Jimmy's heart sank. He opened his mouth to say something but closed it again with a sigh as Ken arrived back with the three lists.

'I'll take the actors,' the Admiral said in his best commanding officer's voice that brooked no argument.

Jimmy nodded resignedly, wincing at the thought of the Admiral interviewing Felicity. 'Very well Sir, then I'd better start with Blake Reynolds' table seeing as you two are not on the best of terms, and we'll aim to meet in the middle.'

Charles Shackleford opened his mouth to argue and for a second Jimmy was worried his former commanding officer was going to pull rank which would have been disastrous. Quickly he thrust the notebook and pen back into the Admiral's hands and said, 'Come on Sir, let's get to it.'

∞∞∞

The Admiral was in his element. He swaggered past Mabel and Emily, only briefly stopping to give them a quick update of the situation – particularly his role in events so far, then, squaring his shoulders, he continued determinedly towards the snug and the cast of the Murder She Spoke Theatrical Company.

All five of the actors were sitting stiffly on the two sofas. The look they gave the Admiral as he entered indicated he didn't have any fans in the room. But that was fine – to his knowledge Charles Shackleford didn't have any fans anywhere…

'Right then you lot,' he said loudly seating himself on the only chair left, 'I'm about to ask you some questions and I'm warning you, I can tell a porky at a thousand paces.' He glared at each of the cast in turn, aiming for the same look he'd admired on *Hercule Poirot* during the Christmas showing of *Murder on the Orient Express*.

'First things first,' he continued when he was sure the cast were suitably intimidated, 'What's your real name Felicity, how do you know Blake Reynolds and when did he give you that shiner under your left eye…?'

Jimmy's interrogating was obviously going a little better than the

Admiral's if the loud voices issuing from the snug were anything to go by.

Biting his lip anxiously, Jimmy wondered what the hell he'd been thinking allowing the Admiral to conduct such sensitive questioning. His old friend was about as sensitive as a frost bitten big toe.

Shaking his head, he paused slightly to centre himself before heading towards Blake Reynolds' and his guests. He couldn't afford to drop a bollock on this one. The chances were that one of the people on this table was their killer...

Three quarters of an hour later the three men reconvened in the entrance hall, seating themselves in the alcove nearest the fire. They each sported a brandy which the Admiral had insisted on for medicinal purposes.

'You go first Ken,' Jimmy said, thinking he'd be best to finish his brandy before the Admiral took centre stage.

'Everyone appears to be accounted for,' said Ken looking down at his notes. 'The head chef and the sous chef didn't leave the kitchen at all during that time period so can both vouch for each other. Richard, the kitchen assistant, was absent for about ten minutes – according to the chef – when he went to the toilet. The waiter and two waitresses were also in the kitchen, except for the times they were taking food into the dining room. I was behind the bar with the two barmen the whole time.'

Jimmy nodded, making a note to question Richard the kitchen assistant further. Finally he turned reluctantly towards the Admiral who was now practically bouncing on his chair. 'How about you Sir?' he asked with trepidation, 'Did you manage to find out if anyone left the dining room during the time frame?'

The Admiral sat forward conspiratorially. 'I think you might be wrong about our murderer being a man, Jimmy lad,' he stated with restrained excitement, 'If you ask me, I think our culprit is none other than Elizabeth Mallery, otherwise known as Felicity. You should see the size of her bloody feet…'

## CHAPTER 11

Mabel and Emily had very quickly got over the thrill at being present during a real live murder mystery and were now plain bored.

They'd exhausted all possible motives for the murder that they could think of and had even written down a list of salient points so they didn't miss anything out when relating the events to Agnes at the WI. The noise in the dining room had increased since the Admiral and Jimmy had finished their questioning, with the majority of it coming from the snug.

'I think Charlie must have used his usual diplomacy when questioning the performers,' observed Emily wryly.

Mabel nodded, completely missing her friend's sarcasm, before glancing towards the dining room doors anxiously. 'I do hope they don't take too much longer, poor old Pickles probably has his legs in plaits by now. He's going to think we've gone off and left him.'

'It wouldn't be the first time,' commented Emily tartly.

'Shall we play a game or something to pass the time?' Mabel asked, suddenly animated, 'I love a good round of hangman.' Emily was about to scoff at the idea when she suddenly remembered she'd brought down her new iPad – she'd been loath to leave it in the bedroom – just in case.

'We could watch tonight's episode of *Britain's Got Talent*,' she said enthusiastically, lifting the device out of her bag.

'How?' Mabel asked doubtfully, 'That finished hours ago.'

'Watch and learn dear,' Emily declared self-importantly, placing the iPad on the table.

'I'm not sure about that Emily.' Mabel shook her head, eyeing the tablet uneasily. 'I once tried to use Tory's computer and I accidently deleted the internet.'

Emily stared at her friend in horror, then looked back down at the iPad. In truth it had been a Christmas present from their daughter. She'd shown Emily how to get something called BBC iPlayer and how to goggle things. But that was all.

Jimmy had messed around with something when they'd first arrived so she'd be able to use it while she was here, but what if he'd managed to delete the internet while he was about it?

Hurriedly, she pressed the buttons as she'd been instructed and breathed a sigh of relief. The internet was still there. She held up the iPad to Mabel and pointed to the little compass. 'See there Mabel, that's Goggle.'

She put the device back on the table, intending to find the BBC thingy, but then she had a brainwave. 'I say Mabel, shall we goggle Darcy DeVine – see if we can find anything interesting?'

'Do you think we should?' Mabel asked excitedly, 'I mean what if someone finds out?'

Emily shook her head, 'Nobody will find out. The internet's on some kind of big spider's web. According to Jim, anybody's allowed to use it.'

A MURDEROUS VALENTINE

Mabel watched eagerly as Emily tapped Darcy DeVine's name into the box. 'Do you think we'll get into trouble?' she asked. Emily shook her head and tapped on the word *images* at the top of the page. Almost instantly a whole raft of pictures appeared on the screen. Looking at each other excitedly, the two matrons prepared to do some research.

∞∞∞

'Sir, I did ask you to confine your questions to where each person was from nine fifteen to ten pm,' Jimmy said through gritted teeth.

'Don't worry Jimmy lad,' the Admiral replied, completely unrepentant, 'I asked that too. Elizabeth was *supposedly* upstairs redoing her make-up.' He looked down at his notes. 'She reckoned she was gone from the room for about fifteen minutes.'

'Did anyone else corroborate that?' Jimmy asked, making his own notes.

'Old Rupert – that's his real name apparently – stated that in his opinion, she wouldn't have had time to kill anybody.' The Admiral shook his head in disdain, making his opinion of the lead actor obvious.

'To be fair, it would've been cutting it fine,' Jimmy responded tapping his pen.

'*That's* if she was telling the truth, which I personally doubt,' the Admiral responded sceptically, 'And Mr. Rupert *Billingford* wouldn't look me in the eye. Bloody shifty if you ask me.'

'So you didn't like him?' Jimmy asked with a frown.

'Couldn't warm to him if we were cremated together,' the Admiral responded bluntly. 'You know the sort Jimmy, all teeth, tits and toenails.'

Jimmy nodded his head thoughtfully. 'What about the rest of the cast? Did anyone else leave the room?'

'They said not,' replied the Admiral. 'Apparently they were *resting* in between performances.'

'And you asked Elizabeth how she knew Blake Reynolds,' Jimmy said brusquely, still smarting from the Admiral's complete disregard of his instructions.

Charles Shackleford shrugged, as usual oblivious to his friend's irritation. 'She said she didn't know what I was talking about,' the large man stated, his scathing tone indicating he didn't believe her for one second. 'Said, of course she'd seen him on the TV but had never actually met him before her performance tonight.'

Jimmy raised his eyebrows and steepled his fingers. 'Interesting,' he mused, 'Why did she lie?' He shook his head perplexed.

'What about the bruise Sir?' he asked, parking the mystery of Elizabeth Mallery's relationship with the producer for the moment.

'Maintained she got it when she slipped in the shower.'

There was a pause as Jimmy jotted down the Admiral's observations

'Right then,' the small man said when he'd finished, 'Did you get anything from anyone else Sir?'

'Only that walker chappy, whathisname?' He glanced down before continuing, 'Mr. Robert Jackson.

'He said he went to bed about eight thirtyish on account of him being knackered from walking nearly five miles in the snow.'

'What was he doing out in this weather?' asked Jimmy curiously.

'One of those nutcase hiker types,' the Admiral responded scornfully, 'You know, idiots who walk miles just for the bloody scenery. He said he got caught out half way between Buckfastleigh and Princetown.' Charles Shackleford gave a theatrical shudder and knocked back the rest of his brandy. 'Bonkers,' he muttered, shaking his head.

Jimmy leaned forward 'That means we've got three people who left the dining room in between nine fifteen and ten.

'When I questioned Mr. Channing, he said he walked with Darcy DeVine as far as the ladies, then went upstairs to his room to get some paracetamol for the actress. According to him, she was complaining of a headache.'

'Not much of a bloody alibi,' muttered the Admiral, 'Did he happen to mention if he'd seen anyone else on his travels? I certainly didn't see him when I went to the heads.'

'No, he said he didn't see anyone,' Jimmy responded neutrally, 'But he did show me the painkillers he supposedly brought down. When Miss DeVine wasn't back at the table, he said he assumed she was taking her time in the ladies.'

'What about the producer?' the Admiral butted in impatiently.

'I was just coming to him Sir. Blake Reynolds said he left the dining room to check on Miss DeVine when he realized she'd been gone quite a long time. According to his statement, he shouted through the door of the ladies, then went up to their suite. When he failed to find her at either location, he returned to the dining room to see if they'd somehow missed one another.'

'So when he saw she wasn't there, why didn't the bloody man raise the alarm?' asked the Admiral brusquely.

'He said she was always wandering off in a sulk,' Jimmy answered. 'Evidently he'd learned to back off and give her space when he thought she needed it.'

The small man paused to gather his thoughts before adding, 'And then there's Elizabeth Mallery who said she went up to her room to repair her make-up.'

'Which she didn't do a very good job of,' the Admiral interjected meaningfully, 'In fact, she didn't look as if she'd put any extra slap on at all. Not to mention the size of her feet... Which you might remember I've already pointed out...'

Jimmy sighed, determined not to rise to the bait. The Admiral was a master at stating his opinion in sixty different ways, until you finally agreed with him out of sheer desperation.

'We also have Richard, the kitchen assistant who went to the toilet, and Mr. Robert Jackson who said he was in bed.

'I think it's time for us to ramp up the heat a little bit gentlemen.'

'I've got a pair of pliers,' offered Ken helpfully…

## CHAPTER 12

The Admiral and Jimmy commandeered the manager's office for their next round of questioning. It was now nearly midnight and Jimmy suggested that before they began interrogating the Suspicious Five, a few sandwiches and some more coffee wouldn't go amiss and actually might well be welcomed by the guests stuck in the dining room.

As Ken hurried off, the two men sat in silence for a while. 'Not quite the romantic evening you were expecting eh Jimmy?' the Admiral murmured eventually. Jimmy grimaced and shook his head.

'It's been so long since I've had to question anybody Sir,' he added after a few seconds. 'I didn't think I'd be able to do it, but it's kind of like riding a bike. I don't think I've ever really forgotten.' He looked over at his former commanding officer. 'I feel like I've used my brain more in the last two hours than in the last fifteen years. Sad really.'

'It'll all be over by tomorrow Jimmy boy,' the Admiral mused after another few minutes of silence. 'We'll be heroes. They might even want to interview us on the TV.' He looked over at the small man sitting slumped in his chair. 'Especially if we solve the murder,' he added excitedly.

'It'll be all over the internet by tomorrow morning,' responded Jimmy despondently. 'There might be a rubbish phone signal here, but the wifi's pretty good. Most of the guests have probably shared the whole bloody cake and arse party on Facebook by now. We'll have half of bloody Fleet Street arriving tomorrow morning along with the plod.'

'But that's tomorrow Jimmy lad,' the Admiral stated decisively. 'Tonight it's our party. It's just you and me Jimmy. And we're going to solve this bloody crime, if it's the last thing we do.'

He stood up, throwing his arms wide and posing melodramatically. 'Let's get to it Jimmy boy, the success of Operation *Murderous Valentine* is in our hands. It's up to us to seek vengeance for the hideous murder of that beautiful young women, Da… Do… De…, the bloody actress. Let's show the boys in blue how it's done.'

A little overcome with the moment, he sat down again, then, after a few seconds of tense silence, turned back towards Jimmy.

'But before we do, could you fetch us a couple of sandwiches and a packet of crisps while I go and get Pickles, I should think his back teeth are floating by now…

∞∞∞

The first of the five to be questioned was Richard, who said his surname was Pounder.

'Bet they called you Dick at school eh?' quipped the Admiral trying to lighten the atmosphere a bit. Unfortunately the witticism was lost on their young suspect who looked as though he wanted to throw himself out of a top floor window.

Jimmy frowned over at the Admiral and the large man subsided sulkily.

'Richard,' Jimmy said, his voice impressively dispassionate, 'You mentioned that you went to the toilet in between nine fifteen and ten. Can you remember the exact time?'

Richard went chalk white as though going to the toilet was a hanging offence. 'I...I... think it was just after nine thirty,' he managed to whisper eventually, 'They were serving the sweet as I left.'

'Did you see anybody?' questioned the Admiral eagerly.

'No...yes...I mean no, I didn't *see* anyone,' Richard stammered after a pause, 'But I *did* hear something.'

The other two men frowned. 'Something, or someone?' Jimmy asked leaning forward.

'I..I don't know...I mean... it must have been someone. It sounded like they were crying.'

'You heard someone crying in the men's toilets?' clarified Jimmy puckering his brow.

'It was more like sniffling really,' responded Richard, warming slightly to his theme. 'As though someone either had a cold, or was trying not to make any noise as they cried. They were in one of the stalls.'

'Did you say anything to them?' asked the Admiral, and Richard shook his head. 'I just figured whoever it was wanted a bit of privacy, and... well, you know... it *was* the gents.'

'Not the best place for opening your heart up, that's for sure,' agreed the Admiral drily.

'So what did you do next?' asked Jimmy doggedly.

'I just did what I had to do - washed my hands and left,' Richard said. 'Whoever it was, was still in the toilet stall when I went.'

'Did you notice which stall the sound was coming from?' Jimmy enquired tensely.

Richard thought for a moment. 'I can't be sure,' he said, 'But I think it was the one on the left. It creeped me out a bit to be honest and I left as soon as I'd finished.'

There was a short silence as Jimmy finished writing notes, only punctuated by Richard's fidgeting, plainly demonstrating his desperate desire to leave.

'Thank you Richard, you've been very helpful.' the small man murmured. 'Err... just one more thing,' he added as the kitchen assistant prepared to make a run for it. 'Could you sign here please?' Jimmy held out the pad he'd been writing on and pointed to the bottom.

At that moment, Richard would probably have signed away everything he owned if it meant he could leg it. Grabbing the pen, he signed hurriedly and two seconds later was out the door.

'Bit of a bloody carry on wouldn't you say?' The Admiral's comment when the two men were finally alone again pretty much summed things up, but didn't really help them much.

'Well, our young friend is left handed, which means he's unlikely to be our murderer,' Jimmy said thoughtfully. 'And the person in the stall had to have been either Ian Channing, Robert Jackson or Blake Reynolds – unless there's someone else we don't know about.'

'Well, I have to say I can't imagine our hard as bloody nails film producer bawling his eyes out in the gents,' commented the Admiral, to which Jimmy shrugged his shoulders.

'You never know Sir. The secret is to keep a completely open mind. Shall we get Mr. Reynolds in next and ask him?'

'Could you go through your movements from nine fifteen to ten pm this evening Sir?' Jimmy asked the producer politely.

Blake Reynolds frowned impatiently. 'I've already told you,' he responded irritably. 'When Darcy went off with her little lap dog, I remained at the table with our other guests. After about twenty minutes Ian came back without her. I asked him where she was and he said he'd left her at the door of the ladies while he went up to his room to get her some painkillers. I remember looking at my watch and commenting that it had taken him a long time to get to his room and back but he just said he'd been using his room's facilities. Obviously too sensitive to use the public ones,' he sneered.

'Were you aware that Darcy and Ian were in a relationship five years ago?' asked Jimmy. Blake Reynolds nodded.

'All very sweet, but at the end of the day, not enough for our Darcy.'

'So why the bloody hell was he invited tonight?' the Admiral interjected bluntly.

The producer looked at the large man with dislike. 'Not that it's any of your damn business,' he stated curtly, 'But Darcy was back to catch up with her family and they bumped into one another. It was she who invited the poor sap. It's the kind of thing she does... sorry... did. Always needed to have people fawning all over her. But she made it pretty damn clear she wasn't interested in him, she just wanted his adoration.'

'So can you remember what time you left the dining room to look for her?' Jimmy questioned, bringing the interview back to the producer's movements.

'It was about five or so minutes after Ian had returned. The stupid man wanted to go back to look for her, but to be honest, I'd had enough of his puppy dog expression so I decided to go myself.

'I opened the door of the ladies and shouted her name but there was no-one there. After that I went upstairs to our suite thinking she'd gone for a lie down, but it was empty.'

'Do you think she could have returned to your suite before going somewhere else?' the Admiral asked astutely causing Jimmy to look over at him in surprise.

Blake Reynolds shook his head and shrugged. 'I don't think so. Nothing had been moved since we came down earlier.'

'So then what did you do?' Jimmy continued.

There was a slight, almost undetectable pause, then, 'I came back down to the dining room because the next act was about to start.'

'Exactly what was your relationship with the deceased?'

Blake Reynolds frowned. 'I would have thought that was obvious.'

'So weren't you worried that something had happened to her?'

'You didn't try very bloody hard to find her,' the Admiral scoffed, 'Was that because you knew where she was…?'

Blake Reynolds got to his feet. 'I don't have to put up with this,' he ground out, stabbing his finger angrily towards the Admiral. 'You're not the bloody police.'

'Sit down Sir,' Jimmy responded calmly. 'We are acting on behalf of the police and it's in your interests to tell us everything you know.'

'Don't you want to find out who your girlfriend's killer was?' added the Admiral bluntly, 'I mean, you don't seem very upset.'

The producer took a deep breath then pursed his lips trying to get his temper under control. After a couple of seconds he sat back down.

'Darcy very often used to go off and hide somewhere…' Blake Reynolds paused and frowned, obviously trying to find the right words. 'There was a… a… darkness about her. You never really knew what she was thinking. Oh, outside, she was all sweetness and light, the perfect Hollywood rags to riches story. But inside…' He paused again. 'Inside, it was though she had something she was hiding from the world.'

'Do you know what it was?' interrupted the Admiral impatiently. Jimmy frowned over at him, expecting the producer's anger to resurface but instead Blake Reynolds leaned back and said ruefully, 'No I never found out – and believe me I tried.'

'Are any of your other guests local?' Jimmy asked suddenly. The producer shook his head.

'No, they're all from London. I suppose they thought it would be amusing to come to the sticks and play murder in the bloody dark.'

'So what made you and Darcy come?'

'It was Darcy's idea. Apparently she used to come here with her parents when she lived in Tavistock. It was her old man's favourite place right up until he died of cancer. To be honest, we couldn't really spare the time for a bloody romp in the country. We were supposed to be flying back to LA tomorrow.'

'Who did Darcy visit while she was down here?' Jimmy asked curiously. The producer shrugged in response. 'Her mother and father both died years ago, but she still has a few cousins living in the area. I can get you their names if you want.'

'Did you fly straight to the west country from Los Angeles?' The Admiral's question was sudden and for some reason seemed to make the producer uncomfortable.

'No,' he answered eventually, 'We were in London for a few days. Darcy had a meeting with her UK agent.'

'Was your visit to Tavistock pre-arranged before you came to England?' Jimmy this time, and again the producer paused.

'Not really. Darcy used to go on about visiting her home town, but never actually did anything about it. Then suddenly she wanted to cut short our time in London and come down to the sticks.'

'Any idea why?'

Blake Reynolds shook his head. 'None at all. Darcy was like that. Mercurial and impulsive.' He sighed, showing emotion for the first time since they'd begun the interview. 'Most of us just had to hang on for the ride.'

His sadness reminded Jimmy of the mysterious crying. 'Did you go to the gents toilets at any time during the time period in question?' Blake Reynolds scowled, his anger returning.

'No I didn't. I've told you my movements and I don't see how else I can help you. Why are you wasting your time questioning me when you could be spending it trying to catch the bastard who did this to her.'

'What's your relationship with Elizabeth Mallery?' Jimmy winced at the suddenness of the Admiral's blunt question, but his eyes remained firmly on the producer. Again there was an infinitesimal pause, then Blake Reynolds shook his head. 'Who is she? I don't know anyone with that name.'

'She's a member of the Murder She Spoke Theatre Company. Tonight, I believe she's going by the name of Felicity.'

The producer stared back at Jimmy, his gaze almost defiant. 'I'm sorry, but I don't know her, so it stands to reason that we don't have any kind of relationship.' His expression turned challenging as he continued, 'She's a bloody good actress though, and now Darcy's left a big hole in Tinseltown, I might be tempted to look her up…'

## CHAPTER 13

As Blake Reynolds left the room, Jimmy showed anger for the first time. 'The man's a complete moron,' he stated bluntly, dragging his fingers through his hair in frustration.

'You're damn right there Jimmy lad,' the Admiral agreed, 'And he's right handed. If he'd been a bit closer he'd have taken my bloody eye out with that finger of his.'

Jimmy sighed. 'So we can't rule him out, and that's apart from the fact that we know he was lying about Elizabeth.'

The small man turned to face the Admiral, his expression hard. 'So why don't we bring her in next, see if we can turn the screws a bit…'

∞∞∞

'Oh Emily,' Mabel said mopping her eyes and finishing her sandwich, 'She was such a beautiful woman. It's all so sad.' They were scrolling through a mountain of pictures showing the actress in various exotic locations. 'She always wore such beautiful clothes. You'd never have thought she was a Devon lass.'

'Look at that one,' Mabel pointed to a group photo which appeared a little different from the rest. Emily tapped on it and the photo suddenly filled the screen.

'It looks as though it was taken somewhere near here,' Emily commented excitedly, 'That's definitely Dartmoor. Which one's Darcy?' The two women pored over the picture showing a large group of laughing young people.

'There,' Mabel said after a couple of minutes, 'That's her, don't you think?' Emily nodded. 'She didn't look much different really, her smile was every bit as dazzling.'

'Who's that next to her?' Mabel pointed at the figure of the man standing next to the young Darcy.

'It looks like Mr. Channing,' Emily said breathlessly. 'He doesn't look very happy does he?' She held the iPad up to the light so they could get a closer look.

'He actually looks angry,' murmured Mabel, 'Perhaps this was taken when they'd just broken up.'

Both women looked over at the man whose heart Darcy had cruelly broken five years earlier. He sat alone with his head in his hands.

Emily tut tutted and narrowed her eyes. 'In my book Mabel, a broken heart is definitely a motive for murder…'

∞∞∞

'Please sit down Miss Mallery,' Jimmy said, pointing to the spare seat. The actress glared at both men then tossed her hair a little dramatically and perched on the edge of the seat, crossing her legs.

Of course the first thing Jimmy noticed was the size of her feet. It had to said they were large for a woman. Any aspirations to a career in Hollywood might well have been tempered by a pair of boats like that. He glanced over at the Admiral who looked back knowingly.

'So, Miss Mallery,' Jimmy continued, looking down at his notes. 'You said you left the snug to repair your make-up. Is that correct?' The actress nodded without speaking.

'Approximately what time was that?' Jimmy asked when it became apparent she wasn't going to offer the information herself.

Elizabeth Mallery threw a nasty look at the Admiral and said, 'Hasn't your gofer told you already?'

'I'd like to hear it from you Miss Mallery, if you'd be so kind,' responded Jimmy mildly.

She sighed loudly and changed her crossed legs in a movement reminiscent of *Basic Instinct*. Fortunately, that's where the similarity ended and Jimmy only just managed to suppress a sigh of relief that she hadn't ditched her underwear.

'I left the dining room at about nine forty and went straight up to my room.'

'Did you see Darcy DeVine on your way up or down?' asked the Admiral. Elizabeth Mallery looked down her nose at him before directing her answer towards Jimmy.

'I didn't see anybody. Like I just said, I simply went upstairs to repair my make-up, then I returned to the snug.'

'What about Blake Reynolds?' the Admiral asked doggedly.

'What is it with the Blake Reynolds thing?' she returned angrily, this time speaking directly to the Admiral. 'Are you more stupid than you look? I told you I don't know the bloody man.'

'Well he knows you,' responded the Admiral, pokerfaced.

The actress fell for the ruse, turning a deep shade of crimson and opening and closing her mouth like a fish.

'What, nothing to say now Miss Mallery?' Jimmy asked calmly as she stared between both men, looking like a hunted animal.

'I suggest you tell us what your relationship is with Mr. Blake Reynolds,' Jimmy continued.

'It's none of your bloody business,' she retorted, her voice angry and defensive.

'We'll decide whether it's our bollocking business or not,' snapped the Admiral, losing his patience. 'So unless you want to be arrested for perverting the course of Justice Miss Mallery, I suggest you bloody well start talking.'

'Well, if you've spoken to Blake, you should already know,' Elizabeth said desperately.

'You know that we've spoken to Mr. Reynolds, but we want to hear it from you now Miss Mallery.' In contrast to the Admiral's bull in a china shop tactics, Jimmy's was the voice of reason.

'How did you get that shiner under your eye,' asked the Admiral as the silence continued. 'Did he give it to you? And don't give me that bollocks about slipping in the shower,' he added as she opened her mouth to answer.

The actress seemed to sag visibly. Her mouth tightened, then she gave a small sob and buried her face in her hands. Jimmy and the Admiral looked at each other silently and waited.

Finally Elizabeth Mallery drew a shaky breath and looked up. Her eyes were swollen and red, and she bit her bottom lip anxiously, obviously trying to work out exactly what they'd been told.

'What would you like to know,' she said at length.

'I suggest you start at the beginning,' Jimmy responded quietly. 'How do you know Blake Reynolds?'

'I met Blake in London, about four years ago,' she murmured eventually, plucking distractedly at the beads on her dress. 'We were lovers. He was going to make me famous.' Her mouth twisted as she looked over at the two men. 'Or at least he was until that mewling little bitch came along.'

'Are you saying he chose Darcy instead of you?' asked Jimmy with a frown.

Elizabeth's lips tightened as she spat out the next sentence. 'He thought she had more *star quality*.'

'Definitely the feet,' thought the Admiral with a sidelong glance at Jimmy.

'Didn't stop him from sleeping with me though did it,' she continued angrily. 'Every time he came to London, he'd call me up, promise me the sodding moon and then bugger off.'

'Why the bloody hell didn't you ditch him if he was such a bastard?' asked the Admiral incredulously, 'Why did you let him use you?'

The actress suddenly deflated. 'I thought if I hung on, he'd tire of Darcy eventually, and then I'd have my chance.' She laughed harshly, 'But instead it was the other way round, the little tart was getting itchy feet. She was looking for a reason to leave Blake behind.'

'Are you saying that Darcy DeVine was about to sever her relationship with Blake Reynolds?' interrupted Jimmy.

'Oh she couldn't just walk away,' Elizabeth smirked, 'That wouldn't look good at all with her precious public. Blake had given her too much. He made her, after all. But she was looking for a way out all the same. She just needed the right reason.'

'And you were going to give it to her,' the Admiral filled in, 'That's why you had the argument in the corridor earlier this evening.'

Elizabeth glanced over at the Admiral in surprise but didn't challenge how he knew about the argument.

'Did Blake Reynolds threaten you Miss Mallery? Is that why you were so scared?'

'He found out that I'd been in touch with Darcy, that we were going to have a little tête-à-tête this weekend.'

'So you saw Blake Reynolds in London earlier this week? And you knew they were coming down to the Two Bridges?'

Elizabeth nodded before laughing bitterly. 'He said he was going to propose to Darcy while they were here. He was so bloody desperate. He knew the little trollop was getting tired of him.'

'How did you manage to wangle your way into the cast of Murder She Spoke?' the Admiral asked curiously.'

The actress shrugged. 'I'm a member of several murder mystery troupes. They were looking for an additional member for this weekend, so here I am.' She held her arms out and shrugged theatrically. 'This is what I'm reduced to. This is what that *bastard* reduced me to. Well, I came down here to give him a taste of his own medicine. Let him know exactly how it feels to be betrayed.'

'Did you manage to have your little chat with Darcy?' Jimmy asked, trying hard to keep his dislike of the actress out of his voice.

Elizabeth shook her head. 'She was supposed to leave me a note at reception, but when I asked, the stupid girl behind the desk told me she'd given it to Blake. That's how he found out.'

'When exactly did he hit you?' questioned the Admiral. 'It was obviously after your argument but before the performance started.'

'Elizabeth stared down at her knees, touching the bruise involuntarily. 'I went looking for Darcy,' she said, raising her head after a few moments, 'I knew I didn't have much time. He... he was so angry when he found out about the note. I saw him go into the bar after we'd finished arguing, and decided to go to their room while he was out of the way.'

She paused and took a deep breath, 'But Blake followed me and dragged me into some kind of cleaning closet. He gave me this and told me if I ever tried to speak with Darcy DeVine again, he'd make me very sorry.'

'So you gave up?'

Elizabeth Mallery laughed mirthlessly. 'God no. I hated him even more after that. I saw Darcy leave her table, so I went upstairs to look for her during the interval. I even went back to her room, but there was no sign of her.

'I was coming back down when I bumped into Blake again. Would you believe he *apologized* for hitting me? I pushed the swine away and went back to the dining room.'

'Did he seem genuinely contrite?'

Elizabeth Mallery stared at Jimmy narrowly. 'I don't think that snake has a remorseful bone in his body,' she spat, 'But I think he was afraid his threats hadn't worked, so thought he'd use his *charm* to persuade me to change my mind about revealing his little indiscretions to Darcy.' She chuckled unpleasantly before adding, 'It doesn't matter now though does it. In the end, she got away from him anyway.'

'What time did you return to the dining room Miss Mallery?' Jimmy interjected, wanting nothing more than to get the obnoxious woman out of the room as soon as possible.'

'It was about five to ten, just before the next act,' she responded carelessly, 'So you see I couldn't possibly have killed little Miss Hollywood. I didn't have the time.'

The actress stood up and stared down her nose at the two men. 'If you've quite finished, I think I'd like to return to the dining room now.'

'Of course,' Jimmy responded placidly, 'Would you mind doing us a favour as you're going that way.' He stood up, went over to the two stacked coffee cups they'd used earlier and held them out towards the actress. 'Could you put these on a spare table in the dining room?'

For a second Jimmy thought she was going to refuse, then, pursing her lips and sighing loudly, Elizabeth Mallery picked them up with her right hand and headed to the door.

'Bollocking hell, I feel like having a shower, just to wash the bloody nastiness away,' muttered the Admiral when the actress had gone out of the room.' Jimmy shuddered and nodded his head in agreement.

'I wonder if she'll tackle Blake Reynolds and discover she's been played,' the small man pondered.

'I doubt it,' the Admiral snorted. 'Our Mr. Reynolds has already clouted her once, and I don't care if he did apologize, underneath all her viciousness, Elizabeth Manning's still scared of him.' He leaned towards Jimmy. 'Do you think she could have done it?'

'Well, she's right handed, and despite what she said, she was away from the dining room long enough, *and* of course as you mentioned Sir, her feet are definitely big enough. But the shoes she's wearing now don't fit the prints. I suppose she could have swapped them over. But at the end of the day what was her motive? Jealousy maybe? But for her plan to work, she needed Darcy alive.'

Jimmy paused and shook his head slowly. 'A vindictive piece of work she maybe, but I don't think she's our killer.'

'What about Blake Reynolds? If what Elizabeth Mallery said was true - that Darcy was set on leaving him - it would certainly give him a motive. Especially if he believed his fortunes were tied in with hers.'

Thoughtfully, Charles Shackleford bent down and gave Pickles a stroke. The elderly spaniel's tail thumped a couple of times on the floor. 'So, who are we going to interview next,' he asked straightening up.

'Let's get Mr. Channing in,' Jimmy mused, 'And see if Darcy DeVine rejected him a second time…'

## CHAPTER 14

'I don't know why she asked me here this evening.' Ian Channing's voice sounded sincere, with just the right amount of bewilderment. 'I saw her in Tavistock. She was surrounded by admirers – it's the first time she's been back since she became famous. I... I was standing on the edge of the crowd and she just looked up and noticed me.' He paused, swallowing convulsively and appeared about to burst into tears.

'She came over and embraced me. Pushed through all those people to get to *me*. Then she put her arms around me and hugged me – in front of everyone. She said she was so happy to see me, that she'd never forgotten me.' He sighed, pausing again before continuing, 'And then she asked me if I wanted to join her here tonight.'

Jimmy and the Admiral looked over at the broken man in front of them. 'Why did you and Darcy split up?' Jimmy asked gently.

Ian Channing shook his head. 'I don't really know,' he whispered at length. 'She just said we'd outgrown each other, that she wanted something better - wanted to change her life.' He frowned before continuing. 'The funny thing was... after we finished, she didn't seem to be doing anything different. Nothing really changed at all – except we weren't together anymore. I thought she'd just used those reasons as an excuse. Then, a few months later, she suddenly vanished.'

'What do you do for a living Sir?' asked Jimmy quietly, trying hard to keep the sympathy out of his voice.

'I'm an estate agent,' Ian Channing murmured before shaking his head ruefully. 'You know for one wonderful second, I thought she might be looking to buy a house back in the area. I thought maybe we would have the chance to get to know one another again.' He repressed a small sob.

'But she soon quashed that idea didn't she Ian?' the Admiral guessed drily.

'She was completely different. She actually laughed at me when I suggested showing her some properties in Tavistock. She asked me why on earth she would ever want to come back to live in a dead hole in the middle of nowhere.

'I was such an idiotic *stupid* fool,' Ian Channing continued, his tone changing to one of self loathing. 'Cloud fucking cuckoo land. And I sat there and let her make a bloody fool of me all over again.'

'So why did you leave the table with her this evening Mr. Channing?' Jimmy asked levelly.

The estate agent shook his head, fumbling for a handkerchief in the pocket of his trousers. 'She asked me to,' he said after blowing his nose.

The Admiral frowned. 'Why?' he asked bluntly, 'I mean if she was making it obvious she had no use for you, why the bloody hell did she ask you to go with her? Where did you think you were going?'

Ian Channing shook his head again, this time with an accompanying shrug of his shoulders. 'She just took my hand and pulled me with her. When we got into the entrance lobby, she let go of my hand and started looking around. It was almost as if she was expecting to meet someone.'

'Did you see anybody?' asked Jimmy eagerly.

'The entrance hall was empty. Or at least I thought it was. She didn't say anything for a minute or so, then she just turned towards me, said she had a headache and asked if I had any painkillers.

'When I said I had some in my room, she begged me to get them for her. She did look very pale,' he added, 'So I told her to stay where she was and I'd be as quick as I could.'

Ian Channing frowned before continuing. 'Darcy said she needed to use the ladies and to take my time. I got the feeling that she'd brought me with her for some particular purpose, then suddenly changed her mind.

'I left her at the door to the ladies and went upstairs to get the tablets from my room. When I came back down to the lobby, she'd gone.'

'Did you search the entrance hall?' the Admiral asked pointedly.

Ian Channing shook his head. 'I just thought she was still powdering her nose, so I decided to pay a quick visit to the loos myself while I waited.'

'Even though you'd already used your room's facilities a few minutes earlier?' questioned Jimmy suspiciously.

'I didn't want to be seen hanging around the bloody place like a lovesick school boy. I mean would you? When I came out, there was still no sign of her, so I went back to the table feeling like a complete imbecile.'

'Did you have a bit of a blub by any chance while you were in the heads?' asked the Admiral directly. The estate agent looked ashamed as he nodded.

'I couldn't help it, I felt as though I'd stepped back five years. Nothing had changed, she still had the same damn hold over me she'd always had.' He stared at the two men despairingly, adding, 'I thought I'd moved on with my life.'

'Did you hear anyone else in the gents while you were there?' asked Jimmy brusquely.

Ian Channing frowned. 'I think someone came in, but to be honest I was too wrapped up in my own misery to pay much attention.'

'Would you like a mint Ian?' asked the Admiral unexpectedly.

Bewildered at the sudden change in the conversation, Ian Channing stared in confusion at the large man as he produced a packet of mint imperials from his pocket and held it out.

'Err… thank you,' the estate agent responded after a couple of seconds, reaching out with his right hand to take a sweet.

'Why did you feel like an idiot Ian?' asked the Admiral abruptly, referring to the estate agent's statement of a few minutes earlier.

Ian Channing's look of despair turned to anger. 'She'd played me,' he snapped after a few seconds, 'Used me to cover some kind of assignation with someone else.' His voice broke, turning once again to sorrow. 'And that someone killed her.'

∞∞∞

'Have you ever been to Tavistock Mabel?' asked Emily as they continued to trawl through picture after picture of Darcy DeVine.

'Can't say I have,' answered Mabel vaguely, staring down at the image in front of her. Emily frowned at her friend's absent minded response and leaned over to see what she was looking at.

It was the picture of a house, or rather what was left of it. The whole thing had been practically burnt to the ground. All that was left was a blackened shell, and the photograph clearly showed the smoke still rising from the ruin.

'It's from a local newspaper article,' Mabel explained in response to Emily's raised eyebrows. 'The Western Morning News. It's dated five years ago. Can you goggle it Emily?'

'Why?' her friend answered, 'Do you think it might be important?'

'I shouldn't think so,' Mabel responded, 'But the house was near Tavistock and the fire happened around the time Darcy left, so it might be worth a quick gander.'

The two women hunched over the iPad as Emily brought up the newspaper report about the fire. The house had been just outside Tavistock. 'That's terrible,' murmured Emily as they read the gruesome details. 'Two people were burnt to death. A husband and wife. How awful.'

'A terrible tragedy,' agreed Mabel, 'The couple were only in their early thirties. What a dreadful waste of young lives.'

'Look there's a picture of them.' Emily pointed at another image. 'Such a handsome couple,' she sighed.

Both ladies stared sadly at the picture, then suddenly Mabel frowned and leaned forward. 'Can you make it bigger?' she asked in a hushed whisper.

∞∞∞

'Mr. Jackson, can you tell me how you came to be at the Two Bridges this evening?' asked Jimmy once their final suspect was seated comfortably.

'Please call me Robert,' was the affable response. Jimmy nodded his head politely and waited.

'I was hiking on the moor and got caught out with the snow.'

'Do you always walk in such bollocking awful weather?' asked the Admiral dubiously.

Robert Jackson turned towards the large man with a grimace. 'The forecast said the snow wouldn't hit until later on tonight. I'd expected to be tucked up nice and warm at my hotel in Buckfastleigh by then.' He spread his arms wide. 'As you can see, I was wrong.'

'What's the name of the hotel you're staying at, err... Robert?' asked Jimmy uncomfortable with the familiarity.

'The White Swan,' responded Robert promptly. 'I have their telephone number here if you'd like to check.'

'So you don't live in the area then?' established the Admiral as Jimmy wrote down the hotel's telephone number. Robert Jackson shook his head.

'As much as I'd like to, my job keeps me in London. I work in the City,' he added by way of explanation. 'Hiking helps me stay sane.'

'If you don't mind me saying so, you look more like a bloody rock singer than a financier,' the Admiral noted, indicating Robert Jackson's thick mop of black hair and well established moustache and beard.

The financier chuckled good-humouredly. 'You've rumbled me,' he smiled, 'I've always wanted to be a singer. Fancied myself as a young Eric Clapton.' He laughed self depreciatingly.

'Were you aware that the actress Darcy DeVine was staying at the Two Bridges this evening?' asked Jimmy.

Robert Jackson shook his head. 'I'd no idea. I saw her very briefly when I was checking in and to be honest I didn't realize who she was. It was only when I was told she'd been murdered that I recognized the name.'

'So you'd never met her before?' queried the Admiral

'Unfortunately not,' answered Robert ruefully. 'I'm afraid we didn't mix in the same circles.'

'Could you tell me where you were between nine fifteen and ten this evening?' asked Jimmy.

'In bed,' responded the financier promptly. 'I was absolutely exhausted after the hellish time I had getting here, and asked for a tray to be brought up to my room. As soon as I'd finished, I went straight to bed which is where I remained until the manager knocked on my bedroom door.'

'Did you hear anything strange?' Jimmy questioned, 'Any noises coming from outside?'

Robert Jackson shook his head. 'My room's on the opposite side to where I'm told you found the body,' he stated, 'And at the time I was dozing to an old episode of *Law and Order*, so it's unlikely I'd have heard anything, even if my room had overlooked the crime scene.'

'What time did your dinner arrive?' asked Jimmy. 'Did you see the person who brought up your tray?'

'It was just before eight, and yes, my meal was brought up by a young lady called Theresa I think. Dark hair, quite well built. Pretty in the healthy kind of way these country girls often are.'

'When I'd finished my meal, I left the tray outside the door.'

'Can you tell us what you had for dinner?' asked Jimmy

'The same as you chaps downstairs I imagine. Soup, chicken and crème brulee. Very nice actually and just what the doctor ordered after a day of strenuous exercise.' He smiled amiably.

'What colour are your pyjamas? The Admiral's question was curt, almost rude, and took both Jimmy and Robert Jackson by surprise.

'If you think I've been wandering the hotel and murdering people in my pjs, I'm afraid you're barking up the wrong tree Admiral Shackleford. I don't actually have any pyjamas - sleep in the buff. You are of course welcome to search my room if you don't believe me.'

'That's very kind of you Sir, we may well take you up on that if you're prepared to sign a statement to say you gave us permission,' responded Jimmy mildly after directing a quick, sharp look at the Admiral. 'We will of course be asking the other guests too.'

Robert Jackson shrugged and nodded, not appearing the least put out by Charles Shackleford's sudden attack. 'Hand me a pen gentlemen and I'll jot something down now,' he offered helpfully.

Jimmy leaned forward and handed the walker a pen and paper. Leaning on the desk, Robert Jackson quickly wrote a statement with his left hand, and signed it with a flourish using his right...

'I hope you find whoever did this,' he said, handing the permission over, together with his room key. 'And please let me know if there's anything else I can do to help.'

'Thank you for your co-operation Mr Jacks... Robert,' responded Jimmy politely, 'We'll certainly let you know.

'I'm sure you must be exhausted,' he added sympathetically, 'But for the time being, we'd appreciate it if you could return to the dining room. I believe there's more hot coffee on offer.'

The Admiral sighed as Robert left the room. 'Well that was pretty damn civilized after all the yelling and shouting. Pity it didn't help us much seeing as our walker appears to be bloody ambidextrous.' He shook his head in frustration.

'I'm going to take Pickles outside again before this damn snow finally entombs us all. I'll be back in a jiffy, then I suppose we'll have to get on with giving Robert Jackson's room a once over before asking the rest of our lovely suspects if we can do the same with theirs.

'Mind you,' he added as he climbed to his feet, 'Could do with another brandy before we start rummaging through any dodgy underwear.'

He was just about to leave the office, when the door burst open to reveal Mabel and Emily fighting to be the first through the opening.

The two men looked at their respective ladies in astonishment, but before either could speak, Emily waved an iPad triumphantly in the air as Mabel whispered breathlessly, 'I think we know who did it…'

## CHAPTER 15

'But how do we prove it?' Jimmy responded ten minutes later. 'We haven't found the murder weapon and we need a motive. It's all pretty much pie in the sky at the moment.' He turned towards the disappointed faces of the two matrons. 'You've done an amazing job, ladies,' he praised, 'But we don't want to get ahead of ourselves and possibly cause the culprit to run. We need to find some hard evidence. Can you two continue digging to see what you come up with?'

Emily and Mabel nodded excitedly. 'We'll keep goggling,' added Emily eagerly. 'What are you and Charlie going to do?'

'We'll head upstairs to Robert Jackson's room and start searching.' Jimmy turned to the Admiral. 'While you take Pickles to ease springs Sir, I'll go and have a quick chat with Ken, see if he can start the ball rolling by asking our other three guests if they'll give us permission to search their rooms.' He shook his head ruefully. 'They might be more amenable to him, but to be honest I can't see any of them falling over themselves to help us.'

'More flannel than a pusser's blanket, the bloody lot of 'em,' muttered the Admiral as he headed towards the door.

'Please don't go anywhere near the body will you Sir?'

Charles Shackleford snorted. 'I've been out there twice already and I'm not likely to drop a bollock like that anyway Jimmy boy,' he answered opening the door. 'I may be new to this Sherlock Holmes stuff, but I didn't get to Admiral simply by being in the wrong place at the wrong time you know.'

The other three stared after him wordlessly. 'I thought that's exactly how he got there,' offered Emily when she was sure he was out of earshot.

'What exactly are we looking for,' asked the Admiral tetchily, pulling on a pair of marigolds. It was now nearly two am and both men were feeling a little worse for wear. Jimmy was still standing in the doorway feeling suddenly overwhelmed.

Perhaps they should just give up and wait for the police to arrive. He looked down at his watch. They'd most likely be here in six hours. The problem was, their culprit might decide to risk the possibility of frost bitten extremities and do a bunk in the mean time. He didn't think any of their suspects really believed he and the Admiral stood any chance of solving the crime, but he didn't think any of them would want to have their dirty laundry aired by the real boys in blue, even if they hadn't been the one to commit murder.

Sighing, he stepped into the room. 'Look for anything you think could have been used as a murder weapon in case our killer's been daft enough to leave it lying around. We've also got that piece of cloth I found tucked behind the drainpipe. We'll hand it over to the forensic chaps when they get here, but it's worth looking to see if any clothing's got a bloody great hole in it.'

"Have we really got to do this for every bollocking room?' the Admiral muttered, looking under the bed half heartedly. 'Come on Jimmy lad, there's got to be a bloody easier way to nail our murderer.' Huffing and puffing, he struggled back to his feet and sat down on the bed.

Sighing, Jimmy sat down beside his friend and picked at his gloves. 'We know the murder weapon was most likely a knife,' he murmured after they'd sat in despondent silence for a few moments. 'The size of the wound was pretty small, indicating that whatever the killer used was narrow.' He paused, thinking. 'Something like a steak knife.'

'Everyone had chicken downstairs and our man Robert reckoned he had the same,' offered the Admiral unhelpfully.

'So where else would we likely find a steak knife, or at least some kind of small thin sharp blade?' asked Jimmy thoughtfully

The Admiral looked over at the small man as though he'd lost the plot. 'In the bloody kitchen of course,' he answered, 'But if we start searching in there, we'll likely still be at when the plods arrive.' He sighed mournfully, 'Let's face it Jimmy lad, I think we're out of our depth here. I went into the kitchen earlier to get that powdery stuff you asked for, and I can tell you it's a bloody murderer's paradise. Knives all over the pl...' The large man stopped and puckered his brow.

Jimmy turned towards him. 'Are you alright Sir?' he asked after a couple of seconds watching the Admiral stare into space.

'We need to go down to the kitchen Jimmy.' Charles Shackleford's voice was hoarse with repressed excitement as he jumped up and hurried towards the door. 'This way Jimmy lad, I know a short cut.'

Although slightly bewildered by his friend's sudden surge of enthusiasm, Jimmy followed the Admiral along a maze of narrow corridors and back stairs without arguing. The one thing he'd learned over the last forty years was that when Charlie Shackleford was on a mission, nothing short of a nuclear bomb would likely stop him. That was probably another reason why he'd made it to Admiral...

A few minutes later the two men burst into the still empty kitchen. Without hesitation, the Admiral hastened over to the other side of the room where the set of tins still sat where he'd left them in front of the block of knives. Hastily moving the tins, the Admiral dragged the block towards the edge of the worktop and stared.

'Look Jimmy,' he pointed as the small man came hurrying up. 'All these knives have the same handle except this one.' Gingerly he pulled out the mismatched knife from one of the slots. Long and thin, it very obviously did not belong to the set. The two men looked at each other, then back at the knife. It had been cleaned but hastily, and there were dark flecks of something around the top of the handle.

'I think you've found it Sir,' breathed Jimmy in awe. 'How the bloody hell did you know it was here?'

The Admiral carefully placed the knife back into the slot. 'It was when you were talking about sharp thin knives, Jimmy,' he whispered elatedly. 'I had to move this block to get at the gravy powder and I remember thinking that one of the knife handles didn't match. Seemed odd to me given that chefs are usually so particular about their equipment.'

Jimmy nodded. 'The murderer must have sneaked in and substituted the correct knife for this one. The only time the kitchen was empty was after we'd moved everyone into the dining room. Our killer must have lingered behind everyone else.' He patted the Admiral energetically on the back. 'Well done Sir, you're a bloody natural at this. I think we should lock this evidence in the manager's office and sit tight until the police get here. We've done our bit and now we deserve that brandy...'

Hurriedly the two men carried the knife block through the entrance lobby towards the manager's office. The area was deserted, the only noise coming from the distant dining room. As they opened the office door, the Admiral suddenly caught a slight movement from the corner of his eye. It had come from the furthest alcove. Halting, he stared into the gloom.

The fire in the large fireplace had practically gone out leaving very little light to penetrate the shadows. For a few seconds he thought he'd imagined it, but no, there it was again. If he stared closely, he could just make out the vague outline of a pair of feet sticking out from the front of a small love seat tucked away round the corner. Somebody was on their hands and knees and they were taking great pains to remain silent and hidden.

There was a slight ripping sound that only someone with excellent hearing would have heard. Fortunately (or unfortunately, depending on who you asked,) the Admiral was famous for never missing a trick.

He turned silently to Jimmy who was looking at him mystified. Whoever it was obviously hadn't clocked them yet so the Admiral put his finger to his lips telling Jimmy to be quiet. Then he pointed towards the unknown person or persons. Jimmy took a step forward and peered into the darkness. After a couple of seconds he nodded and the Admiral mimed that they should go and investigate.

Carefully the two men tiptoed towards the indistinct crouching figure. They left the office door slightly ajar to give them at least a small amount of light by which to navigate the shadowy assault course and they managed to avoid falling over anything right up until they were a few feet away.

Stopping and turning towards Jimmy, the Admiral pointed towards their oblivious quarry and mimed that he intended to surprise the person by executing well timed rugby tackle. At least that's what Jimmy thought the Admiral's gyrating movements were telling him. Either that or his friend was impersonating Elvis.

Frantically Jimmy shook his head, miming a downward stabbing motion with his right hand and clutching at his neck with his left. It was obvious the small man thought their quarry could be dangerous. There was a killer at large who'd already half inched one knife – why not two?

The Admiral threw his hands in the air. This, together with a hurriedly mimed chicken indicated his frustration with his friend's lily livered attitude. However, before their actions had chance to morph into a rendition of Shakespeare's Macbeth, fate took the matter out of their hands as the door to the dining room opened, followed by the sound of footsteps hurrying through the bar towards the lobby.

Immediately the feet in front of the sofa stilled and the two hunters froze.

'Jimmy, Charlie, are you there? I think we've finally found something to nail the killer …'

Unfortunately neither Mabel nor Emily had ever had the opportunity to get to grips with the finer points of surveillance gathering and had definitely been watching too many episodes of Hawaii Five O. Their voices were loud enough to alert even the deafest murderer, especially if the culprit happened to be hiding in the same room.

As the two ladies pushed open the office door, everything seemed to happen at once. The feet disappeared as the suspected killer jumped up and spotted the Admiral and Jimmy for the first time.

'Don't move,' yelled the Admiral grabbing hold of the nearest heavy object and thrusting it towards the figure in front of him. Unfortunately the object happened to be a statue of Atlas holding up a bronze model of the World.

As the Admiral threw out his arm, the globe shot forwards like a cannon ball and only narrowly missed giving the shadowy figure an impromptu lobotomy. As it was, the ball hit the suspect's shoulder eliciting a muffled oomph as whoever it was toppled backwards onto a strategically placed coffee table.

The noise of the splintering furniture brought out the feisty side of Pickles, usually well buried along with the fetching of balls and sticks. The Springer shot out of the office and raced towards the prone figure, all the while barking as though his last role had been in a re-run of Lassie.

The Admiral and Jimmy watched in astonishment as Pickles hurtled past them and launched himself onto the prone figure. 'Great bollocking Scott,' breathed the Admiral in horror, visions of his elderly spaniel suddenly turning into *Cujo* and tearing their victim limb from limb. A couple of seconds later, he breathed a sigh of relief as Pickles' tail started wagging, and the Springer proceeded to deploy a more effective weapon - licking the suspect into submission.

## CHAPTER 16

It was safe to say that Detective Chief Inspector Barratt was either very impressed by their investigative skills, or just deliriously happy that he hadn't had to shovel his way across the wilds of Dartmoor at stupid o'clock in the morning. By the time the forensic team had arrived, all that remained of the crime scene was an indistinct mound of snow. If Darcy DeVine hadn't been spotted when she was, the outcome might have been very different.

The body was removed, and evidence catalogued, and all that remained was for DCI Barratt to give his comb over a quick tidy up and assure the media, even now camped outside in the Two Bridges car park that the heinous murder of actress Darcy DeVine had been solved and a suspect arrested.

The culprit was led away in handcuffs, leaving Charles Shackleford and Jimmy Noon to join the Chief Inspector for a well-earned wobbly coffee to fill in the blanks.

By the time they'd managed to pull Pickles off, the prone figure was shouting his guilt hysterically, anything to prevent the monster seated on top of him making a snack out of his nose.

With Pickles growling theatrically every time he so much as moved, Robert Jackson was more than willing to come clean.

It turned out that his real name was John Dickinson. He had supposedly died in the fire that killed his wife and consumed his home five years earlier. It turned out he'd also been having an affair with the then Darcy Hopewell, which was the real reason Darcy had finished her relationship with Ian Channing.

Apparently, John wanted to leave his wife, but due to a pre-nuptial agreement with his much wealthier spouse, he would be left penniless should he be stupid enough to do so.

Even then Darcy aspired to the finer things in life, and that didn't include tying herself to a impoverished insurance salesman. So together they hatched a plan to remove John's wife from the picture permanently.

According to their suspect, Darcy had been instrumental in driving the plot to murder his wife, and as he witnessed her single-minded callousness, John claimed he actually began to fear for his own welfare should he ever outlive his usefulness. So, unbeknown to his lover, he began to make plans of his own.

Obviously a much better insurance salesman than he'd been given credit, John Dickinson created a false persona to claim on a life insurance policy on the event of his death. When he started the fire that killed his wife, John also made sure that it looked as if he'd perished in the house with her.

Believing her lover to be dead and fearing that someone might discover her own involvement, Darcy Hopewell fled to stay with an old friend in California. Once there she quickly put her past behind her and Darcy DeVine was born.

John Dickinson made his way to London where he took the name of Robert Jackson and made a new life for himself.

That was until the unfortunate day when he bumped into the now famous actress. Despite cultivating copious amounts of facial hair to effectively change his appearance, Darcy had recognized her former lover. Any idea he might have harboured of her letting bygones be bygones, went up in smoke as soon as he received the letter she went to great lengths to have hand delivered to his office.

She demanded he return to their old stomping ground to meet with her or she would reveal his continued existence to the appropriate authorities. At first John hadn't been too worried. If she chose to tell the world he was still alive, she risked implicating herself in the whole sordid affair. He knew that she didn't need his money, so in his arrogance believed she simply wanted to see him again – perhaps she was still in love with him, even after five years.

It took less than thirty seconds to completely disabuse him of that notion. The look she'd cast him as he'd been checking in earlier spoke of a level of hatred that took his breath away. From that moment he knew his only way out was to remove her – permanently.

He might have got away with it too if Emily and Mabel hadn't been conducting their own unique brand of sleuthing and recognized him as being the man in the article about the burned house. John Dickinson's disguise was not quite as good as he'd thought, or perhaps he'd just got careless.

What was Darcy DeVine's motive for taking Ian Channing along with her when she'd left the dining room to meet her former lover? Perhaps she had a premonition that John Dickinson would refuse play her games, whatever they were, and wanted Ian for insurance - hoping that he would recognize the face under the beard too.

But for whatever reason, she decided against involving the estate agent at the last minute, which may well have saved his life…

That left one last question. Why on earth had their suspect been on his hands and knees in a tucked away corner of the hotel lobby? If he'd hoped to conceal himself until the weather improved enough for him to make a run for it, his choice of hiding place certainly left a lot to be desired.

However, a quick search underneath the small sofa John Dickinson had been crouching at quickly revealed what he'd been up to. Obviously believing the Admiral and Jimmy would be occupied for at least half an hour futilely searching his bedroom, the murderer had waited out of sight until he saw them go upstairs, then taken the opportunity to hide the trousers he'd been wearing when he'd stabbed Darcy DeVine.

Not only were they missing a large piece of fabric in the knee, but they were dotted with the blood of the victim. After temporarily hiding them behind the curtain on his way to the dining room earlier, John Dickinson had sought a more permanent hiding place within the lining of the sofa.

Jimmy spread his hands indicating there was very little more to tell. 'We think John Dickinson also hid the murder weapon somewhere in the lobby when he was first asked to come downstairs, and most likely transferred the knife to the kitchen on his way to be interviewed. It was only Charlie's observational skills and quick thinking that led us to its hiding place.

'But as to why on earth Darcy DeVine decided to meet her killer outside on such a freezing cold night without any additional layers, we'll never know,' the small man finished, 'All we can guess is that she didn't want to waste the time it would take to go and fetch a coat.'

'As it was,' the Admiral interrupted, I only just missed bumping into the pair of them in the lobby.' He puffed up a little before continuing, 'As Jimmy mentioned, my uncanny observational skills and quick thinking led me to follow the actress and her ex when they left the dining room. Unfortunately, I mistakenly believed the pair to be in the bar, so by the time I got into the entrance lobby, there was no sign of them. If only I'd stepped outside...'

Charles Shackleford sighed with genuine regret as DCI Barratt snapped shut his notebook and leaned forward to drink the last of his coffee.

'I'd like to thank you both for your sterling efforts in this case, gentlemen,' the detective said with a satisfied nod. 'Without your hard work, we may well have missed any opportunity to apprehend the culprit. All that remains is to ask if you would both attend Crownhill police Station in Plymouth to give a statement. Tomorrow will do.'

The three men stood and shook hands. 'I won't take up any more of your time gentlemen, please pass on my thanks and good wishes to your lovely ladies.'

∞∞∞

'I don't think I've ever had such an exciting Valentine's evening,' said Mabel over a complimentary cream tea in the hotel bar later on that day.

Emily shuddered slightly. 'A little too bloodthirsty for my taste,' she mumbled round a large scone liberally coated with jam and clotted cream.

'All very satisfactory I'd say,' added the Admiral, popping the last of his scone into his mouth with a contented belch. 'This dit will give us free drinks for the next month at the Ship. We'll be celebrities Jimmy boy.'

The small man looked over at the Admiral and shook his head. His former commanding officer never ceased to amaze him. 'I shouldn't think Darcy DeVine will have quite the same thoughts on the matter, wherever she is,' he murmured reproachfully.

The Admiral leaned back, Jimmy's mild reprimand as usual like water off a duck's back. 'We make a bloody good team Jimmy lad,' he said, 'Look how smoothly an operation goes when you follow orders.'

He was completely oblivious to the amazed expressions of the other three as he leaned back and steepled his fingers contemplatively. In his head, he'd already solved Darcy DeVine's murder single-handedly.

'*The case of the Murderous Valentine,*' he mused thoughtfully after a few seconds. 'You know what Jimmy lad? I think we could be on a roll…'

## THE END

Book Two of The Admiral Shackleford Mysteries: A Murderous Marriage and Book Three: A Murderous Season are now available on Amazon.

Of course, if you haven't yet read the Shackleford Diaries and would like to know just how the Admiral was instrumental in getting his daughter Victory hitched to the most famous actor in the world, not to mention the 'little shenanigans' with the Thai prostitute and Bible Basher Boris… all seven books in the series are available on Amazon.

*Book 1 - Claiming Victory*
*Book 2 - Sweet Victory*
*Book 3 - All for Victory*
*Book 4 - Chasing Victory*
*Book 5 - Lasting Victory*
*Book 6 - A Shackleford Victory*
*Book 7 - Final Victory*

Continue reading to the end for an exclusive sneak peek of Claiming Victory, Book One of The Shackleford Diaries…

# AUTHOR'S NOTE

Dartmoor National Park is a vast moorland in the county of Devon, in southwest England. Ponies roam its craggy landscape, defined by forests, rivers, wetlands and rock formations (tors). Trails wind through valleys with Neolithic tombs, Bronze Age stone circles and abandoned medieval farmhouses. The area has a handful of villages, including Princetown, home to Dartmoor Prison, used during the Napoleonic Wars.

For more information go to:

https://www.visitdartmoor.co.uk

If you happen to be in the area, please make sure you visit, it's beautiful and wild and one of my favourite places on earth.

And while you're there, you can visit the Two Bridges hotel… Yes it really does exist and has a very special place in my heart because my husband and I got married there…

Perched on the banks of the beautiful West Dart River, it's a lovely old

BEVERLEY WATTS

historic coaching inn with roaring log fires, first class food , gorgeous bedrooms and delicious locally brewed ale…

You can find out more by visiting their website:

https://www.twobridges.co.uk

# KEEPING IN TOUCH

Thank you so much for reading A Murderous Valentine, I really hope you enjoyed it.
For any of you who'd like to connect, I'd really love to hear from you. Feel free to contact me via my facebook page: https://www.facebook.com/beverleywattsromanticcomedyauthor or my website: http://www.beverleywatts.com.
If you'd like me to let you know as soon as my next book is available, sign up to my newsletter by copying and pasting the link below and I'll keep you updated about all my latest releases.
https://motivated-teacher-3299.ck.page/143a008c18

Thanks a million for taking the time to read this story. As I mentioned earlier, if you've not yet had your fill of the Admiral's meddling, you might be interested to read the next two instalments of *The Admiral Shackleford Mysteries.*

Book Two: *A Murderous Marriage* and Book Three*: A Murderous Season* are all available on Amazon.

You might also be interested to learn that the Admiral's Great, Great,

Great, Great Grandfather appears in my series of lighthearted Regency Romantic Comedies entitled The Shackleford Sisters.

Book One: *Grace*, Book Two: *Temperance*, Book Three: *Faith*, Book Four: *Hope*, Book Five: *Patience*, Book Six: *Charity*, Book Seven: *Chastity,* Book Eight: *Prudence* and Book Nine: *Anthony* are currently available on Amazon.

And lastly… if you haven't read them yet but think you'd like to give The Shackleford Diaries a go, turn the page for an exclusive sneak peek of *Claiming Victory*, Book One…

# CLAIMING VICTORY

*Chapter One*

Retired Admiral, Charles Shackleford, entered the dimly lit interior of his favourite watering hole. Once inside, he waited a second for his eyes to adjust, and glanced around to check that his ageing Springer spaniel was already seated beside his stool at the bar. Pickles had disappeared into the undergrowth half a mile back, as they walked along the wooded trail high above the picturesque River Dart. The scent of some poor unfortunate rabbit had caught his still youthful nose. The Admiral was not unduly worried; this was a regular occurrence, and Pickles knew his way to the Ship Inn better than his master.

Satisfied that all was as it should be for a Friday lunchtime, Admiral Shackleford waved to the other regulars, and made his way to his customary seat at the bar where his long standing, and long suffering friend, Jimmy Noon, was already halfway down his first pint.

'You're a bit late today Sir,' observed Jimmy, after saluting his former commanding officer smartly.

Charles Shackleford grunted as he heaved his ample bottom onto the bar stool. 'Got bloody waylaid by that bossy daughter of mine.' He sighed dramatically before taking a long draft of his pint of real ale, which was ready and waiting for him. 'Damn bee in her bonnet since she found out about my relationship with Mabel Pomfrey. Of course, I told her to mind her own bloody business, but it has to be said that the cat's out of the bag, and no mistake.'

He stared gloomily down into his pint. 'She said it cast aspersions on her poor mother's memory. But what she doesn't understand Jimmy, is that I'm still a man in my prime. I've got needs. I mean look at me – why can't she see that I'm still a fine figure of a man, and any woman would be more than happy to shack up with me.'

Abruptly, the Admiral turned towards his friend so the light shone directly onto his face and leaned forward. 'Come on then man, tell me you agree.'

Jimmy took a deep breath as he dubiously regarded the watery eyes, thread veined cheeks, and larger than average nose no more than six inches in front of him

However, before he could come up with a suitably acceptable reply that wouldn't result in him standing to attention for the next four hours in front of the Admiral's dishwasher, the Admiral turned away, either indicating it was purely a rhetorical question, or he genuinely couldn't comprehend that anyone could possibly regard him as less than a prime catch.

Jimmy sighed with relief. He really hadn't got time this afternoon to do dishwasher duty as he'd agreed to take his wife shopping. Although to be fair, a four hour stint in front of an electrical appliance at the Admiral's house, with Tory sneaking him tea and biscuits, was actually preferable to four hours trailing after his wife in Marks and Spencer's. He didn't think his wife would see it that way though. Emily Noon had enough trouble understanding her husband's tolerance towards 'that dinosaur's' eccentricities as it was.

Of course, Emily wasn't aware that only the quick thinking of the dinosaur in question had, early on in their naval career, saved her husband from a potentially horrible fate involving a Thai prostitute who'd actually turned out to be a man...

As far as Jimmy was concerned, Admiral Shackleford was his Commanding Officer, and always would be, and if that involved such idiosyncrasies as presenting himself in front of a dishwasher with headphones on, saluting and saying, 'Dishwasher manned and ready sir.' Then four hours later, saluting again while saying, 'Dishwasher secured,' so be it.

It was a small price to pay... He leaned towards his morose friend and patted him on the back, showing a little manly support (acceptable, even from subordinates), while murmuring, 'Don't worry about it too much Sir. Tory's a sensible girl. She'll come round eventually – you know she wants you to be happy.' The Admiral's only response was an inelegant snort, so Jimmy ceased his patting, and went back to his pint.

Both men gazed into their drinks for a few minutes, as if all the answers would be found in the amber depths.

'What she needs is a man.' Jimmy's abrupt observation drew another rude snort, this one even louder.

'Who do you suggest? She's not interested in anyone. Says there's no one in Dartmouth she'd give house room to, and believe me I've tried. When she's not giving me grief, she spends all her time in that bloody gallery with all those airy fairy types. Can't imagine any one of them climbing her rigging. Not one set of balls between 'em.' Jimmy chuckled at the Admiral's description of Tory's testosterone challenged male friends.

'She's not ugly though,' Charles Shackleford mused, still staring into his drink. 'She might have an arse the size of an aircraft carrier, but she's got her mother's top half which balances it out nicely.'

'Aye, she's built a bit broad across the beam,' Jimmy agreed nodding his head.

'And then there's this bloody film crew. I haven't told her yet.' Jimmy frowned at the abrupt change of subject, and shot a puzzled glance over to the Admiral.

'Film crew? What film crew?'

Charles Shackleford looked back irritably. 'Come on Jimmy, get a grip. I'm talking about that group of nancies coming to film at the house next month. I must have mentioned it.'

Jimmy simply shook his head in bewilderment.

Frowning at his friend's obtuseness, the Admiral went on, 'You know, what's that bloody film they're making at the moment – big blockbuster everyone's talking about?'

'What, you mean The Bridegroom?'

'That's the one. Seems like they were looking for a large house overlooking the River Dart. Think they were hoping for Greenway, you know, Agatha Christie's place, but then they spied "the Admiralty" and said it was spot on. Paying me a packet they are. Coming next week.'

Jimmy stared at his former commanding officer with something approaching pity. 'And you've arranged all this without telling Tory?'

'None of her bloody business,' the Admiral blustered, banging his now empty pint glass on the bar, and waving at the barmaid for a refill. 'She's out most of the time anyway.'

Jimmy shook his head in disbelief. 'When are you going to tell her?'

'Was going to do it this morning, but then this business with Mabel came up so I scarpered. Last I saw she was taking that bloody little mongrel of hers out for a walk. Hoping she'll walk off her temper.' His tone indicated he considered there was more likelihood of hell freezing over.

'Is Noah Westbrook coming?' said Jimmy, suddenly sensing a bit of gossip he could pass on to Emily.

'Noah who?' was the Admiral's bewildered response.

'Noah Westbrook. Come on Sir, you must know him. He's the most famous actor in the world. Women go completely gaga over him. If nothing else, that should make Tory happy.'

The Admiral stared at him thoughtfully. 'What's he look like, this Noah West... chappy?'

The barmaid, who had been unashamedly listening to the whole conversation, couldn't contain herself any longer and, thrusting a glossy magazine under the Admiral's nose, said breathlessly, 'Like this. He looks like this.'

The full colour photograph was that of a naked man lounging on a sofa, with only a towel protecting his modesty, together with the caption "Noah Westbrook, officially voted the sexiest man on the planet."

Admiral Charles Shackleford stared pensively down at the picture in front of him. 'So this Noah chap – he's in this film is he?'

'He's got the lead role.' The bar maid actually twittered causing the Admiral to look up in irritation – bloody woman must be fifty if she's a day. Shooting her a withering look, he went back to the magazine, and read the beginning of the article inside.

*"Noah Westbrook is to be filming in the South West of England over the next month, causing a sudden flurry of bookings to hotels and guest houses in the South Devon area."*

The Admiral continued to stare at the photo, the germination of an idea tiptoeing around the edges of his brain. Glancing up, he discovered he was the subject of scrutiny from not just the barmaid, but now the whole pub was waiting with baited breath to hear what he was going to say next.

The Admiral's eyes narrowed as the beginnings of a plan slowly began taking shape, but he needed to keep it under wraps. Looking around at his rapt audience, he feigned nonchalance. 'Don't think Noah Westbrook was mentioned at all in the correspondence. Think he must be filming somewhere else.'

Then, without saying anything further, he downed the rest of his drink, and climbed laboriously off his stool.

'Coming Jimmy, Pickles?' His tone was deceptively casual which fooled Jimmy not at all, and, sensing something momentous afoot, the smaller man swiftly finished his pint. In his haste to follow the Admiral out of the door, he only narrowly avoided falling over Pickles who, completely unappreciative of the need for urgency, was sitting in the middle of the floor, scratching unconcernedly behind his ear.

Once outside, the Admiral didn't bother waiting for his dog, secure in the knowledge that someone would let the elderly spaniel out before he got too far down the road. Instead, he took hold of Jimmy's arm, and dragged him out of earshot – just in case anyone was listening.

In complete contrast to his mood on arrival, Charles Shackleford was now grinning from ear to ear. 'That's it. I've finally got a plan,' he hissed to his bewildered friend. 'I'm going to get her married off.'

'Who to?' asked Jimmy confused.

'Don't be so bloody slow Jimmy. To him of course. The actor chappy, Noah Westbrook. According to that magazine, women everywhere fall over themselves for him. Even Victory won't be able to resist him.'

Jimmy opened his mouth but nothing came out. He stared in complete disbelief as the Admiral went on. 'Then she'll move out, and Mabel can move in. Simple.'

Pickles came ambling up as Jimmy finally found his voice. 'So, let me get this straight Sir. Your plan is to somehow get Noah Westbrook, the most famous actor on the entire planet to fall in love with your daughter Victory, who we both love dearly, but - and please don't take offence Sir - who you yourself admit is built generously across the aft, and whose face is unlikely to launch the Dartmouth ferry, let alone a thousand ships.'

The Admiral frowned. 'Well admittedly, I've not worked out the finer details, but that's about the sum of it. What do you think…?'

*Claiming Victory is available from Amazon*

Turn the page for a full list of all my books available on Amazon.

# ALSO AVAILABLE BY BEVERLEY WATTS ON AMAZON

**The Shackleford Diaries:**
Book 1 - Claiming Victory
Book 2 - Sweet Victory
Book 3 - All For Victory
Book 4 - Chasing Victory
Book 5 - Lasting Victory
Book 6 - A Shackleford Victory
Book 7 - Final Victory

**The Admiral Shackleford Mysteries**
Book 1 - A Murderous Valentine
Book 2 - A Murderous Marriage
Book 3 - A Murderous Season

**The Shackleford Sisters**
Book 1 - Grace
Book 2 - Temperance
Book 3 - Faith
Book 4 - Hope
Book 5 - Patience

*Book 6 - Charity*
*Book 7 - Chastity*
*Book 8 - Prudence*
*Book 9 - Anthony*

**The Shackleford Legacies**
*Book 1 - Jennifer*
*Book 2 - Mercedes*
*Book 3 - Roseanna will be released on March 27th 2025*

**Standalone Titles**
*An Officer and a Gentleman Wanted*

# ABOUT THE AUTHOR

**Beverley Watts**

Beverley spent 8 years teaching English as a Foreign Language to International Military Students in Britannia Royal Naval College, the Royal Navy's premier officer training establishment in the UK. She says that in the whole 8 years there was never a dull moment and many of her wonderful experiences at the College were not only memorable but were most definitely 'the stuff of fiction.' Her debut novel An Officer And A Gentleman Wanted is very loosely based on her adventures at the College.

Beverley particularly enjoys writing books that make people laugh and currently she has three series of Romantic Comedies, both contemporary and historical, as well as a humorous cosy mystery series under her belt.

She lives with her husband in an apartment overlooking the sea on the beautiful English Riviera. Between them they have 3 adult children and two gorgeous grandchildren plus 3 Romanian rescue dogs of indeterminate breed called Florence, Trixie, and Lizzie. Until recently, they also had an adorable 'Chichon" named Dotty who was the inspiration for Dotty in The Shackleford Diaries.

You can find out more about Beverley's books at www.beverley-watts.com

Printed in Great Britain
by Amazon